KURT'S WAR

The Boy Who Knew Too Much

David Canford

In memory of my father, who was evacuated out of London as a child for the duration of the Second World War.

COPYRIGHT © 2019 DAVID CANFORD

This novel is a work of fiction and a product of the author's imagination. Any resemblance to anyone living or dead (save for named historical figures) or any entity or legal person is purely coincidental and unintended.

2.23

Cover Design By: Mary Ann Dujardin

CHAPTER 1

When Kurt found the letter, his world changed. Letter was probably too grand a term for the crumpled piece of paper which he found tucked away in the back of a drawer in the sideboard to keep it hidden from prying eyes. His prying eyes. Torn from a notepad that his father must have used at work, it consisted of only one line, short and to the point.

Gone back to Germany. Our marriage is over.

The previous week his mother had given her son an entirely different explanation.

"Your father's firm told him he needed to go to Germany to sort out an order."

That had sounded plausible. He worked for a German-owned company which imported its equipment into the United Kingdom.

"How long for?"

"A few months, maybe."

"A few months! Why didn't he tell me before he went."

"It came up unexpectedly. He had to rush home in the middle of the day and pack his things while you were at school to get to the boat in time."

Despite his words of protest, Kurt wasn't close to his father. Otto Ziegler wasn't an approachable character. A man of few words and quick to lose his temper, he demanded total obedience from his only child. They never did anything fun together. The only time which Otto paid any attention to his son was on Sunday afternoons when he would insist that Kurt remain indoors and study German. From outside, Kurt would hear shouts of excitement and the thud of a leather ball. He yearned to go and play with the other boys, but his father was impervious to his pleas.

"I'm giving you something worthwhile. The gift of another language, and not just any language. Germany is set to be Europe's powerhouse. Speaking German will give you a tremendous advantage in life. When those urchins out there grow up, they'll still be living right here with dead-end jobs. You, however, fluent in German will be able to make something of yourself and leave them far behind."

Kurt used to wonder why, if speaking German was such an advantage, that his parents lived where they did. It hadn't made his father a fortune, but he knew better than to mention that or he'd probably feel the stinging pain from being thrashed with the man's belt.

Although unsure whether he even liked his father, Kurt had been unhappy that he would just leave without saying goodbye. Now that Kurt knew the truth, the hurt was worse. His father couldn't have loved him, not one bit. The man hadn't even bothered to leave his son a note, or an address, nothing at all. Kurt's father was never coming back, vanished as if he had never existed.

"What's that you've got there?" His mother stood at the doorway to the small dining room with its three china ducks in flight displayed in a diagonal line on the wall in the fashion of the times. "Don't try and hide it. Show me."

Her expression changed from one of accusation to sympathy when she took the piece of paper from him.

"Come here." She held out her arms. "I'm sorry I hid it from you. I thought it would be easier for you that way. I intended to give you time to get used to him being away before telling you." Her voice faltered as she stroked his hair.

Kurt looked up at her with his big, soulful eyes. "Don't worry, mum. I'll take care of you. I'll get a job after school, and I can find one for Saturdays too."

"That's very sweet of you, darling, but your education is more important, and there's absolutely no need. I'll put a camp bed up in my room for you, and we can rent out your room to a single lady. What with that and my sewing machine, I'll be able to make enough to make ends meet. Now, why don't you run along and play until tea time."

Kurt knew that he loved his mother. She was the

opposite of his disciplinarian father, from whose forehead a frown had rarely been absent. Audrey Ziegler smiled and laughed often. Her son couldn't understand why his parents had married each other. He could see why his father would have been attracted to his mother, but why she had fallen for his dad was a mystery.

The summer sun was still high in the sky as Kurt opened the front door, although the seasons weren't much in evidence here in London's Docklands. Brick and concrete were the local vegetation. Trees were few and far between in this land of identical houses, all joined to one another. Behind them, the cranes at the docks loomed upwards as if the limbs of some gigantic, many tentacled ferrous creature lying in wait for any child who dared to get too close.

When Billy Smith saw him approaching, he put his hand up and the rest of the boys stopped kicking the football they were playing with on the road between the two rows of houses. Billy was the eldest and tallest, and towered over Kurt.

"What do you want, Ziegler?" He pronounced the name slowly and deliberately, almost hissing to emphasise its difference, widening his mouth and showing his missing front tooth as he did so.

"I just wanted to join in. Which side do you want me on?"

"Neither. Dad says there'll be a war with Germany soon so you can bugger off. We don't want no Nazis in our game." Kurt didn't move. "Did you hear what I said? Sod off or I'll rearrange that ugly face of yours."

The other boys watched intently, gleeful at the possibility of a fight. Knowing that he wouldn't win, Kurt put his hands in his pockets and sloped off as slowly as he thought he could get away with without inviting retaliation. He'd been bullied at school for having a German father. Memories of the Great War were still fresh in the minds of parents who moulded their children's view of the world. Lately though, things had got worse.

He resented his father. Not only had he abandoned them, he had also left a legacy which his son would never be free from. German blood ran in his veins. The boys' parents probably remembered his father marching with Mosley's blackshirts, the British Union of Fascists, and their anti-Jewish and anti-communist rallies, and the street fights with those groups. Doubtless, they would conveniently have forgotten that some of the other fathers had participated in the same marches at one time.

Although not quite eleven years old, Kurt knew something significant was about to happen. Everyone at school had already been issued with gas masks. The pupils had all thought it great fun at first when they were told to put them on. With the black rubber covering their faces, a perspex eye-strip to see through, and the large protruding filter by their chins, they looked like a cross between deep sea divers and alien monsters.

It had become even more amusing when the

children discovered that by blowing out through the rubber, they could make a farting sound. The novelty would soon wear off, however. The masks were hot and smelly, and unpleasant to wear for any length of time.

"Quiet. Children, be quiet!" their teacher had bellowed above the cacophony of forty children all laughing and shouting at the same time. "You may take them off now. But remember to look after them, and keep them with you at all times in the cardboard box they came in."

"Why do we need them, Miss?" one of the girls had asked.

"In case there's a war with Germany, Deidre. They might use gas to try and kill people. The masks will protect you. The canisters contain charcoal which will soak up the poison."

"Kurt's a German," one of the boys had cried out.

"No, I'm not. I'm British. My father's German, not me."

"Well, if he's a German, that makes you a kraut."

"Boys, do stop squabbling. I don't want to hear another word."

The teacher hadn't sought to defend Kurt, and the damage had been done. Many of Kurt's classmates treated him differently after that. He had never had many friends. Now he didn't have any apart from Craig. A boy who was teased each time he opened his mouth because he spoke with a broad Glaswegian accent, his family having recently moved down from Scotland. However, at least that meant he was prepared to hang around with Kurt.

CHAPTER 2

It seemed that Billy Smith's father might be right. On the last Saturday of August 1939, Kurt's mother told him that she had to go to the school for a meeting.

"What for?" demanded Kurt.

"It's to explain what's going to happen in the case of evacuation."

"Evacu what?"

"If there's a war, which there may well not be, it'll be safer to leave London for the countryside."

"That sounds nice. We've never been to the country."

His mother was back after an hour. Kurt, who'd been standing on the sofa by the front window so that he could see her coming, jumped down before she could notice. Their sofa was a sacred object. He wasn't even supposed to sit on it, let alone climb on it. He raced to open the front door, eager to find out more.

"I've got a long list of what you'll need to take with you. Do you want to help me get your things ready?"

"What about what you'll need?"

"It's only the children who'll be going. Mums and dads will be staying here. But there's no need to worry, you'll be staying with a lovely family I'm sure of it, and all your school pals will be in the same place."

Kurt's face collapsed like a poorly cooked soufflé.

"I'm not going. I don't want to go without you."

"It'll only be for a short while."

"That's what you said when dad went away. I don't believe you."

"Kurt-"

But he'd already begun running up the stairs, slamming the door to his bedroom shut as he got there. He flung himself face down onto his bed, his eyes wet as he fought to hold back the tears. Kurt didn't want to be sent away, not if his mother wasn't coming. She was his refuge. He hated school, being rejected because of who his father was. If a war started, they'd hate him even more.

His mother came in and sat down on the bed.

"I only want you to be safe."

"I will be. Why can't I stay? There might never be a war you said. And if there is, there might not be any fighting here. Please." His mother said nothing. Kurt pressed his case. "Can't we wait and see what happens? You can send me later if there's trouble. Say yes, mum, please."

Audrey Ziegler looked at her boy, her hands clasped together with indecision and torment. He was the image of her with his hazel eyes, his brown hair, and the way he showed his teeth when he smiled. Apart from the bump in his nose and small ears, he didn't look at all like her husband.

No mother wanted to be separated from her child. He was all that she had left. Her parents were dead and Audrey had no siblings. Without Kurt, a tunnel of loneliness stretched out before her with no light at the end of it. The neighbours had never been friendly towards her. They would whisper behind her back, criticising her choice of husband on more than one occasion. Sometimes they would have a dig at her to her face as she stopped to say hello when they were gathered together on the street gossiping, throwing their words around themselves like barbed wire.

"Evil people the Huns."

"I couldn't agree more. And that Hitler they've got running the country now, he'll do it all again if we give him half a chance. It beggars belief that any self-respecting woman would have married one of them."

Their folded arms and long stares would tell Audrey that she wasn't welcome.

Audrey put her hand on Kurt's shoulder. "All right, you can stay in London for now."

"Thanks, mum," said Kurt flinging his arms around her.

On the last day of August, the government gave orders for Operation Pied Piper to commence the following day. The code word was not publicly disclosed at the time when officials realised that the name was an unfortunate choice in current circumstances, the same as that of a German folk tale, and one which didn't end well for the children concerned. The authorities' intuition to proceed proved well founded. The very next day, Germany invaded Poland and Britain issued an ultimatum demanding that Germany withdraw.

At school that day, Kurt and the others whose parents had decided not to evacuate their children, were told to sit quietly in their classrooms as all the teachers would be busy assisting those who were leaving.

There were only a few kids left in his class. Kurt was pleased to see that those who had been the ringleaders in bullying him weren't amongst them. Contrary to instructions to remain seated and read their books, the children went over to the window to watch. Outside, the evacuees had been assembled. Like a group of orphans, they had a cardboard label on a piece of string hanging from their necks with their name and address. Some had small suitcases, others rucksacks, and a few only a pillow case slung over their shoulder for transporting their clothes. They also carried a cardboard box containing their gas masks. Each of them clutched a paper bag with the standard issue of a bar of chocolate, an orange, and raisins for the journey.

A small number looked excited but the majority appeared overwhelmed by the occasion as mothers waved by the school gates, putting on a brave face for the sake of their children. In no time at all they had been organised into single file and were off, marching towards the station. The headmaster led the procession as if he were indeed the Pied Piper of Hamelin, taking the children away because he hadn't been paid for ridding the locality of a plague of rats. Once the children were out of sight, the mothers hugged each other for comfort as they wept. Everyone was still reeling from the shock that only twenty years after the last war with Germany, supposedly a war to end all wars, another one now seemed inevitable.

Over the next three days, more than a million were moved out of the cities identified as being most at risk with London top of the list. It was to be a momentous weekend. That Friday night, the street lights didn't come on when it got dark. On Saturday, Kurt's mother came home from shopping carrying a long roll of black material.

"What's that for?" asked Kurt.

"To make blackout curtains so that at night if the Germans fly over, they won't know where they are. It'll be as if London's disappeared into thin air."

Come evening, Kurt couldn't resist peeping out through the curtains. The moon silhouetted clouds scudding across the sky. He had never witnessed his city in complete darkness. It was scary yet in a thrilling sort of way.

"Come away from the window!" shouted his mother as she entered his room. "You'll have the

Air Raid Wardens knocking on our door. I can't afford to be fined. If you want to look out, you need to turn your light out first."

Kurt used to enjoy being out after dark. He didn't want to be out anymore once he had tried it under the new circumstances, at least not on his own. Overnight, London had become a different place, one of unlit streets, and alleyways as black as a coal mine. A place where you could hear buses yet not see them until they passed in front of your nose, the passengers sitting motionless in the darkness like corpses from an underworld who only came alive at night.

Sunday dawned as a glorious late summer day, one which seemed destined to be blissfully warm and care free. Walking the streets with his friend Craig, Kurt was astonished to see what appeared to be numerous bulbous, silver-coloured airships rise into the sky as they walked along by the River Thames towards Tower Bridge and the Tower of London.

"What on earth do you think those things are?"

"Barrage balloons," said Craig. "My father says it's to stop enemy planes dive bombing. They'd hit the steel cables that hold the balloons in place and crash."

It was as if London had become a life size cover for a science fiction novel.

When Kurt arrived home, his mother was sitting by the radio, dabbing her eyes with a handkerchief.

The man's voice was clipped and rather chilling. Kurt caught only the end of the broadcast.

"That was the Prime Minister. We're at war with Germany."

"Does that mean we're at war with dad?"

"No, of course not."

"But he went back to Germany."

"Yes, but it's the German government we're fighting, not your father."

Kurt didn't really understand the difference. Before he could say anything further, sirens sounded and his mother leapt to her feet and grabbed his hand so hard that it hurt.

"We'll hide in the cupboard under the stairs." It was dark and cramped like in a game of hide and seek but without any of the fun. Kurt bit his lip as they crouched down, expecting an explosion to light up and shatter his world at any moment. He needn't have worried, the all clear was given almost as soon as they got in there.

"That's a relief, it must have been a false alarm. Time to put the kettle on, I'm spitting feathers," said Audrey Ziegler.

CHAPTER 3

When Kurt got home from school one afternoon the following week, a woman who he didn't recognise was sitting at the dining table sipping a cup of tea.

"Kurt, this is Miss Dorfmann. She's going to be lodging with us. I have explained that your father's in the army. Miss Dorfmann's from Germany too. She hates Hitler, just like he does."

His mother gave Kurt an intense stare which he readily understood meant not to say anything which would contradict her story.

"Pleased to meet you, Kurt," said the woman as she held out her hand for him to shake. She was much younger than his mother with crimped black hair and bright red lipstick. He liked her smile. Kurt thought she looked as glamorous as a film star even if her dress was plain and a dark navy in colour.

Although it was odd at first to have a stranger in the house, Kurt soon became accustomed to it. Miss Dorfmann was almost as invisible as air. She worked long hours, and most of the time when she was home, she stayed in her room. On the few occasions that she spent the evening in the living room with them, her presence was a calming one. She would read while his mother sewed, altering and mending clothes for other people to earn money.

It was only a few days after her arrival that there was a confident knock on the front door late one afternoon. Kurt ran to open it. He was still just of an age when everything was worth running for. Kurt's enthusiasm shrivelled into trepidation when he saw the local policeman standing there. Kurt hoped that he hadn't come to arrest him for breaking the blackout earlier that month.

"Is your father in, sonny?"

Kurt stepped back. This adult was intimidating, a giant of a man with the deepest of voices. The local kids would all flee if they were up to no good when they heard the metal heel protectors on the soles of his shoes resounding off the pavement.

"Who is it? Oh, do come in Constable," said his mother as she appeared from the kitchen, wiping her hands on her apron. "Is something the matter?"

"I need to take your husband down to the station. They're interning enemy aliens who might constitute a threat to national security."

"I'm afraid you're too late. He left us and returned to Germany some weeks ago."

"Did he now." The policeman stroked his chin a

couple of times, considering what to do next faced with this unanticipated news. "Do you mind if I take a look around? It's not that I don't believe you, but Sarge down at the station will give me a right rollicking when I get back if I don't."

"No, please go ahead. We've nothing to hide."

They waited in the hallway while he toured the house, noisily opening cupboards and shutting doors. He then clomped down the stairs in a manner for which Kurt would have been reprimanded

"Just as you said. Though I couldn't help noticing that there were some books in German in the bedroom with the single bed."

"They belong to our lodger. Miss Dorfmann. She loathes Hitler, that's why she's come over here."

"Miss Dorfmann," he repeated, taking out his notepad and pencil from the breast pocket of his uniform to write down the name. "I'll need to check that she's registered with us. If there's any problem, I'll be back. Thanks for your help, Mrs. Ziegler."

Months passed and the war never arrived. By the New Year, over half the children evacuated at the end of the summer had returned. Kurt asked one of the boys at school what it had been like.

"Stinky. The whole village smelled of pig shit coming off the farms."

"What about the family you stayed with?"

"Nice enough but I'm glad to be back home."

Rationing began and posters encouraged people to dig for victory. Kurt didn't know how he and his mother could. Their small backyard was covered in concrete. He got used to eating bread without butter. The weekly allowance was only two ounces. Kurt's main worry was that they might limit the amount of sweets which he was able to buy. That really would be a hardship difficult to bear.

Occasionally, Kurt would try to imagine what his father was doing, and whether he had joined the German army to fight against England. Most of the time, however, he never thought about him. Kurt didn't miss him.

One night as Kurt went up to bed, he noticed that the door to Miss Dorfmann's room was ajar. She was sitting on her bed with her back to him, holding something. It sounded as if she might be crying. Kurt backed away but the creaking of a floorboard as he did so caused her to turn her head. Her eyes were red around the edges.

Kurt felt obliged to ask how she was. "Are you all right?"

She forced a smile. "I'm fine, thank you. I was looking at a picture of my family. Did you want to see them?"

Kurt wasn't bothered but knew it would seem rude to say no.

"That's my mother and father, and my brother, Jakob. And me of course."

It was a formal portrait, the parents were seated, their two children standing behind them. They were rigid and uncomfortable looking as they posed. Their photographer hadn't captured any of the love that existed between them.

"Why don't they join you here?"

"They used the money which they had to pay for me to come to England. I'm saving as much as I can from what I earn to send to them so that they can leave Germany, if they will still be allowed to that is. You must miss your father too."

"Mm," was all Kurt could manage. "Goodnight then."

Sitting on his bed back in his room, Kurt had an idea. Shaking the money out of his piggy bank, he counted it. Five pennies. Keeping one to buy some sweets, he crossed the hallway and knocked on the now closed door.

"Yes?" asked Miss Dorfmann as she opened it.

"I know it's not much but I've got four pennies. I want you to have them to help your family get here."

As he held out his hand, she looked as if she might be about to cry again. Kurt hoped not as he wouldn't know what to do.

"Oh, that's so kind of you, Kurt. Thank you so much. That will help a great deal."

Kurt turned to go.

"Wait. Do you play chess?" asked Miss Dorfmann.

"No."

"Well, tomorrow evening if you like, I'll teach you.

I have a chess set. One which my father made for me."

"All right."

Kurt went to bed thinking that she was lucky to have such a father. His own had never made anything for him.

Most evenings after that he and Miss Dorfmann played at least a couple of games. The first time that Kurt won, or as Kurt decided when he thought about it in later years when Miss Dorfman had let him win, she produced a bar of chocolate.

"A prize to celebrate your first victory."

One afternoon, Kurt came home from school to an unfamiliar noise. His mother was standing by the back door watching a man with a pick axe hacking away at the concrete.

"That's Mr. Williams. He's converting the yard into a vegetable garden for me," said Audrey Ziegler in response to her son's inquisitive look. "Isn't that kind of him? Maybe you could help. Hey, Bill, this is Kurt. Is there anything he can do to lend a hand?"

The man, who was built like an ox and had hands the size of plates, stood up straight and wiped his forearm across his brow to remove the sweat, leaving a smear of dirt across it in the process.

"He can pick up the pieces of concrete and put them in my wheelbarrow."

Bill didn't say anything to the boy as he helped. He didn't even look at Kurt. Later, his mother emerged from the kitchen with a jam sandwich for each of them. Kurt sat on the doorstep to eat while the adults stood chatting and laughing.

At the end of the evening, the concrete was gone, and by the end of the following week, a proper vegetable garden had been planted. His mother was overjoyed, extolling Bill and his efforts but Kurt wasn't thrilled in the least. He didn't consider the prospect of having more vegetables to eat as something to be pleased about.

In May 1940, the so-called Phoney War came to an end when Hitler invaded France. Britain's beaten army withdrew from the beaches of Dunkirk. Adults spoke quietly when children were about, yet they could sense something serious was afoot.

"I overheard mum and dad talking last night," said Craig, poking his stick of liquorice into his sherbet fountain while the two boys walked along the street kicking an empty tin can which they'd come across. "They say now France is beaten, Hitler will try and invade Britain."

Kurt wondered if his father would be involved, and whether he might come marching down their street. The boy had mixed feelings. Germany was the enemy, however the boys who had been nasty to him wouldn't dare be like that any longer if his father reappeared as part of a conquering army. Even if his father didn't return with the invasion force, those boys would soon shut up about him having a German father should Britain fall.

On the brick wall which he and his friend were

passing, a poster had been put up. It pictured a boy with his arms around his sister, proclaiming 'Mother, send them out of London'. Kurt hoped that he wouldn't be sent away. After all, there still hadn't been any attacks on the city.

In the days which followed, the children who had returned after the evacuation at the start of the war left London again, accompanied by many of those who hadn't gone the first time. Much to Kurt's relief, he wasn't among them.

As well as the evacuees, Miss Dorfmann also disappeared.

"The government's interning all Germans now, even refugees," his mother explained when he asked where she was when she didn't return from work as usual.

"Refugees?"

"Those who have had to flee their country because of persecution. Though I don't for the life of me understand why people like her have been taken."

"Taken where?"

"To camps, while the government works out who's dangerous and who's not, I suppose. Maybe she'll be released soon but she'll have lost that job of hers. It's such a pity. Now she won't have the money to send to her family so they can escape."

Kurt was sad that she'd gone. He had liked her, and worse than that he'd have no one to play chess with.

That summer, there were few children in the

streets of Kurt's age. It didn't concern him that much however. He was already used to being alone.

It was another perfect September day, a Saturday, when it began. Kurt was outside in the late afternoon sunshine. A distant murmuring caught his attention. Looking east, he could see a mass of dark shapes inexorably heading his way like a swarm of locusts. The murmuring became an intense buzzing. Open mouthed, he stood transfixed at the sight, not even moving when the bombs began to fall. Ear shattering explosions followed, jets of water erupted from the Thames, and dockside cranes and warehouses collapsed.

"Come inside!" His mother jerked him out of his trance and pulled him indoors and into the cupboard under the stairs. This time it was no false alarm. He shut his eyes tight as china falling off the dresser shattered on the floor and the entire house shook. Kurt shook too.

The Battle of Britain had already been raging in the skies of Southern England for two months, but it had been a distant thing to Kurt. Germany's attacks were focused on airfields and other military installations. Frustrated at lack of a quick victory, Hitler had ordered a change of tactic. That day marked the first day of the Blitz. Over three hundred bombers and six hundred fighter planes in a formation many miles wide brought the war to the nation's heart. It was the biggest bombing raid the world had seen.

That night, guided by flames from the fires which the afternoon's raid had created, the Luftwaffe returned. This time Kurt and his mother went to the nearest Underground station to shelter. Rats were scurrying around the streets seeking to escape the infernos, and in the air was the incongruous sweet smell of caramel from barges carrying sugar which had caught fire earlier.

Subterranean nights became normal. Upon hearing the siren, he and his mother would hurry to the Underground with hundreds of others. Initially, Kurt found it all rather exciting. An adventure. He wasn't perturbed by the whiff of all that humanity crammed together on the platform, and the almost suffocating heat which came from being down there with so many.

They would take a blanket to lie on, but it wouldn't be until the early hours that he got any sleep. There was almost a party atmosphere. People playing cards and other singing songs. Briefly, worries were forgotten in this surreal world far beneath the pavements of London.

Returning bleary-eyed to the surface early morning was a shocking contrast, worse than waking up with a hangover if Kurt had had any comprehension of what such a thing was. Fires were still burning, and smoke blocked out the rising sun. Only the distinctive dome of St. Paul's Cathedral stood above it all, like a mirage. Where once buildings had been, mountains of rubble and bomb craters had taken their place.

Previously only rain had fallen from the sky. Now death poured down from it too. Soon Kurt became accustomed to the new reality. What he never got used to, however, were the shouts and screams of those still trapped, or the crushed and mangled bodies pulled from the wreckage. His mother warned him not to look but the first time he couldn't resist the urge. He regretted ignoring her advice.

When his school took a direct hit, Kurt and Craig got to roam the streets of London for the day. They soon forgot the destruction around them. Their eyes had fixated on pieces of shrapnel, glinting like buried treasure. They didn't need to say anything, they both understood its potential. Something to impress the other boys at their new school, wherever that might be.

"Hey, Craig. Come and look at this. I've found a piece with German writing on it. Craig?"

Kurt turned to see what was keeping his friend. Craig, who had been rummaging in some rubble across the street, was illuminated by a blinding flash and blown backwards through the air. Adults ran to his aid.

"Let me through, I'm his friend."

Kurt pushed his way past the small crowd and burst into tears when he saw the boy. An air raid warden walked him home and accepted his mother's offer of a cup of tea. When he left, she came up to her son's bedroom.

"It's too dangerous here for you. I need to send you

out of London so that you can be safe."
This time Kurt didn't resist.

CHAPTER 4

His mother came to the station to wave him off. Those children who were to be evacuated had already gone. Kurt would be travelling alone and was being sent to a different part of the country to those from his school. That didn't concern him, on the contrary he saw it as an advantage. He'd be safe from the bullies.

"Look after your ration book and identity card. I'll be down to see you as soon as I can," shouted his mother as the train began moving along the platform. Smoke coming from the engine soon obscured her as she melted into it.

In a few miles, city sprawl gave way to fields and hedgerows. Apart from the occasional town, that was all there was. Kurt had only ever left London before to go to the seaside. That had been but a short journey east. This time, going west, the distance seemed endless. Although surrounded by other passengers, Kurt felt alone. Most of them would be heading home to the reassurance of familiarity. He, on the other hand, had left the only place which he had ever known to go and live with complete strangers. It was a daunting prospect and he sunk lower in his seat.

At each stop, Kurt listened for the guard shouting out where they were. All nameplates had been taken down to confuse the enemy in case of invasion. Likewise, all road signs had been removed. Changing onto a smaller train for the last stage of his journey, it was late afternoon when he arrived at Brushford, the station for Dulverton. The small town in Somerset close to the border with Devon that was his destination. As he stepped down from the train, a woman in a hat with a pheasant's feather in it and a fox fur draped around the shoulders of her green coat came over to him. Kurt thought the poor fox looked rather sad. The lady, however, seemed extremely jolly with a sympathetic face and a voice which sounded as if it might break into laughter at any moment.

"Are you Kurt?" He nodded. "Good, you made it then. I'm Mrs Bishop, the vicar's wife. Everyone laughs at that but it is rather appropriate, don't you think? And if my husband's promoted, he'll be Bishop Bishop." She chortled. "Well, I expect you've had a long day. My car's just outside the station. I'll drive you into Dulverton. It's a two mile walk otherwise."

Kurt had never been in a car before. Not many people owned one at that time. He wondered how a vicar's wife could afford to buy one.

Dulverton was in a valley. Kurt had never seen a

place like it, hemmed in by hills. To him, they were the fortress of his isolation. As they approached a bridge with low walls of stone crossing the river below it, Mrs. Bishop swung the steering wheel sharply to the left.

"That's Dulverton town centre, such as it is, across the bridge, but we're going up here to Miss Althorpe's where you'll be staying."

The road, if it could be called that, was barely wide enough for the car and extremely steep. They parked in the driveway of a large house. It was painted white and half-timbered in wood stained black. Behind the house, forest climbed upwards to the skyline, and below them lay the town as if viewed from a bird's nest. Miss Althorpe must be rich to live here, thought Kurt.

Mrs. Bishop knocked on the door with gusto.

"Good afternoon, Miss Althorpe." The woman opening it didn't return her greeting. Instead, she looked rather annoyed that she had visitors. "This is the boy-"

"I've already told you that I don't want anyone. I'm no good with children, and I don't like them. You'll have to find someone else to take him in."

She shut the door in their faces. Mrs. Bishop rolled her eyes at Kurt and knocked again, repeatedly, until it re-opened.

"I'm afraid you have no choice. There's a war on if you haven't noticed. We all have to make sacrifices and play our part, and you'll be paid for it. Most families around here have taken children in, and they don't have all the room that you do. Now, will you take this boy or do I have to report you to the police?"

Both women stood glaring at each other, like boxers facing off before a fight. Kurt hoped Miss Althorpe would refuse to back down and then he might get to go with Mrs. Bishop who seemed nice, or if not her, at least a family who might be more welcoming. However, it was Miss Althorpe who blinked first.

"All right then, I'll do it."

"Thank you."

"It's under duress, mind you."

"Kurt, be at school tomorrow morning. Miss Althorpe will be able to tell you how to get there. I'm sure you'll soon make lots of friends. I'm afraid that I have to dash but do come to church on Sunday and we can talk further. Toodle loo."

Miss Althorpe jerked her head back in a grudging indication that Kurt could enter. Her face was severe. A tall, thin woman, she was dressed in a tweed jacket and skirt, and white blouse. He couldn't discern anything pleasant about her. He wondered if she even knew how to smile. She seemed as buttoned up as her jacket. After the sunshine outside, the interior of the house folded around him, dark and oppressive.

"Kurt. That's an unusual name." Her tone was cold and authoritarian.

"My father's German."

"I imagine that's raised a few eyebrows. Well, I

won't hold that against you. I don't take to children full stop. It doesn't matter to me what nationality they are. This room, as you can see, is the kitchen where you can help yourself to water or make a cup of tea. I won't be cooking for you, so make sure you eat your school lunches. If you're hungry, you can help yourself to an egg from the hen house in the back garden. I assume that your mother will have taught you how to boil an egg. Just remember to close the coop so that the foxes don't get in. The bread is in the bread bin over there, and there's milk in the pantry. Follow me and I'll show you to your bedroom."

She led him down a corridor, up the staircase, and along another corridor. The dark brown of the parquet flooring and deep green of the wallpaper sucked up most of the limited light which came through the latticed windows.

"Your room." She opened the door and stood back so that Kurt could enter. "Your bathroom's next door. You can have one bath a week, no more. And don't fill it any higher than the line marked around the bath. Except when you're coming in and out, I don't want to see you. You are to stay put in your bedroom. Apart from the kitchen, the rest of this house is out of bounds. And never come in through the front door, only use the one at the side which you arrived at. Do you understand, boy?"

"Yes." His reply was almost inaudible.

"Speak up. I can't abide mumbling."

"Yes!"

"And I don't like shouting either. Obey my rules and don't give me cause to have to discipline you. Cross me and you'll wish that you hadn't."

When she went back downstairs, Kurt put his small suitcase and the cardboard box containing his gas mask on the single bed and took off the label hanging from his neck. He had never felt so wretched and insignificant. This must be what it was like to be an orphan, unloved and unwanted. In an effort to cheer himself up, he told himself that at least here he might make some friends at school.

That night the darkness was ominous. In London, there might no longer be street lights but the night wasn't so completely dominant. There were people out walking and the sound of traffic. Here, apart from the hooting of owls and the occasional screeching, which Kurt later discovered came from foxes, the silence was uninterrupted and total. It spooked him.

When a bat flew in through his open window flapping like a winged vampire, Kurt was terrified. It went around and around the room while he cowered on the floor, convinced that it would land on his head and bite him. As soon as the creature found its way out, he shut the window and never opened it again.

CHAPTER 5

School in Dulverton was divided by a fault line: the local kids and the evacuees, all of whom, apart from Kurt, had come from the city of Bristol. Kurt fell in the crack, belonging to neither tribe. To him, both contingents had a strange way of speaking. Those born in Dulverton spoke with a Somerset accent (or 'Zummerzet' to be more precise). Those evacuated there had the Bristolian twang with its long 'o's and 'r's, and dropped 't's'. Everyone considered his London accent a source of merriment. But that wasn't the only reason why he was teased and shunned in the playground.

"Class, this is Kurt Ziegler from London. I want you to make him welcome," the teacher, a Miss Bridges, announced on the morning of his arrival.

There was a sudden loud boom, then another. Instinctively, Kurt threw himself under the desk.

"It's all right, Kurt. You can come out. We don't have air raids here, it's just the army up on Exmoor practising their firing."

The other pupils were laughing at him. Keeping his glance firmly downwards, Kurt could feel himself turning the colour of a beetroot as he sat back down.

The children soon put two and two together. He wasn't only a boy who spoke "funny" and who had a foreign name, he was infected with German genes. Once again, he didn't fit in. "Kurt the Kraut" and "Hitler's poodle" were just two of the names the other kids would taunt him with. This time he had no welcoming refuge to retreat to at the end of the day. Back at the house, Miss Althorpe avoided him. On the odd occasion that they passed in the corridor, she said nothing unless she had a complaint to make which she often did.

"I expect you to wash up any plates which you use, not leave them on the side. I'm not your housekeeper. And another thing, remember to take your shoes off when you come in. I had to clean your muddy footprints off the floor the other day. I won't warn you again."

There were a few pleasures to be found in his new environment. He enjoyed being sent to a nearby farm to collect milk, which was so fresh that it was still warm. Kurt would drink some straight from the milk can and eat blackberries which he picked from the bushes as he went along, being careful to wipe off the telltale signs of white and purple from around his mouth before entering the house. When Miss Althorpe was out, he would go into the garden and open the rabbit hutch, taking out one of the rabbits which she reared for food. Stroking its fur while he cuddled it in his arms would make him feel happy.

As an only child, and one who had never had many friends, Kurt could cope with his own company better than most. The first weekend he went exploring, making his way up the River Barle. It was one of those uplifting days. The sky was a joyous uninterrupted blue that could make even a sad person smile and dispersed the grey clouds of Kurt's mind. The trees, tall and wide, decades if not centuries old, were at the peak of their autumn colour, vibrant with attractive shades of yellow and orange. In the light breeze leaves drifted languidly and silently down to earth. Those already fallen made a pleasing crunch beneath Kurt's boots. As he went along he enjoyed the novelty of kicking the leaves into the air, a new experience for the boy. His concrete streets of London's East End had been bereft of trees where nature was smothered under asphalt.

After a few miles, he reached a bridge the likes of which he had never seen in London. Tarr Steps was an ancient clapper bridge. Large flat slabs of stone, supported at intervals by vertical ones, traversed the river as though stepping stones for a giant. Today, only the very top of them were visible with the water lapping against them after the heavy rains of yesterday.

Kurt sat down nearby and took the sandwich which he had made for himself from the cardboard box that had once held his gas mask. There was nothing around here, he'd decided, that could be remotely worthwhile for the Germans to bomb, and so there seemed little point carrying the mask around everywhere he went as he had done in London.

While he ate, he watched a horse coming down the steep track bordered by hedges on the other side of the river. It was very different to the huge horses that Kurt had seen pulling the milk carts in London, or the majestic beasts of the King's Household Cavalry, ridden by soldiers in their red cloaks and shiny helmets of silver and gold the time when he had gone with his mother to watch the changing of the guard at Buckingham Palace. This horse appeared primitive and stunted by comparison. It was stocky with short legs and looked too small for the girl about his age who was riding it. Kurt thought that they might fall off the bridge into the fast flowing water as they crossed. At one point the horse stopped and reared its head in protest, but the rider clearly knew how to handle the animal.

"Hello, don't I know you?" she said coming to a halt beside him.

Close up, the horse was intimidating for a city boy. Kurt leapt to his feet and backed away.

"Maybe. I go to the school in Dulverton."

"Ah, yes. That's where I've seen you. The boy who hangs around on his own. I don't blame you. Personally, I prefer the company of animals to people. Animals accept us for who we are. What's your name?"

"Kurt."

"Barbara. People call me Barb. Aren't you the one with the German dad?" Kurt nodded. "That must be hard. The idiots at school don't understand that the war's not your fault."

Kurt immediately took a liking to her. She wasn't judging him just because of his ancestry.

"What kind of horse is it?"

Its coat was brown save for a circle of oatmeal colour around its mouth and nostrils, and black fur on the lower half of its legs.

"It's a she. Bella. She's an Exmoor Pony. Most of them live wild up on Exmoor, which starts just behind these hills. They're in terrible danger right now what with Exmoor being used by the army. Many are being injured or killed. It's such a terrible shame. I worry there'll be none left if the war goes on for much longer. It's one of our oldest breeds and man could wipe it out. Sometimes I feel like going up there to round up as many as I can and bring them down to safety."

"Teacher says we mustn't or we'll be blown to pieces."

"I know. Where are you living?"

"Miss Althorpe's."

"Poor you. She seems a right miserable old cow. I live at the farm a mile or so out of Dulverton. You must have passed it on the way here. Anyway, I ought to be going. Bye."

Kurt opened his mouth to say goodbye but she

had already trotted off. When he got back, early evening was casting long shadows. Miss Althorpe's motor car had gone from the driveway.

Entering the house, curiosity got the better of him. At the end of the corridor beyond the staircase which led to his bedroom was a door which Kurt had been forbidden to go through. He turned the handle. The corridor continued. The doors to the first two rooms were open, a dining room and a study. The last door was shut. Kurt opened it and walked in. It was the living room.

The walls were panelled with wood which gave it a sombre appearance in common with the rest of the house. Spotting a framed photograph on a small table next to an armchair, Kurt went over and picked it up. Written at a diagonal near the bottom were the words:

"To my dearest Mabel."

The man in the frame was unlike anyone who Kurt had ever seen. He wore a military uniform and sported a long black moustache. Almost as wide as his face, it curled upwards at either end like the flamboyant signature of a monarch. Although the picture was black and white, the man's skin was clearly dark in tone. Returning the frame to the table, Kurt walked around the room looking for other objects which might shed some light on the background of the woman whose roof he lived under.

Three ornamental brass elephants stood trunk to tail on the sideboard. He picked one up and found it surprisingly heavy. Kurt was careful to put it back in the same spot. He didn't want the old bat to know that he'd been in the room or he would most certainly be in serious trouble.

On the walls, hung paintings of what appeared at first glance to be humans. Closer examination revealed that they had other attributes. One was of a man seated whose nose was an elephant's trunk, another a woman surrounded by flames. Her tongue was red and her skin grey. Around her neck hung a garland. Kurt leaned forward for a closer look and drew back in horror. Attached to the garland were shrunken decapitated heads.

Unnerved, Kurt quickly left before looking at the remainder of the pictures. He had no idea what it all meant but resolved to keep to his part of the house in future. Miss Althorpe had become an even more intimidating figure.

CHAPTER 6

In late November, his mother paid a visit. He met her at the bus stop by the bridge.

"Kurt, my darling boy." He moved back as she advanced to hug him. Two boys from school were passing by. He didn't need to be labelled 'a mummy's boy' on top of everything else. "How have you been? I must say you've got a good colour in your cheeks. It must be all this fresh country air, though you do look rather thin. I expect you're having a growth spurt. Look at you. You're as tall as I am." Excited at seeing her son again and to be in Dulverton, she hardly paused for breath. "My, what a pretty little town this looks. Are you going to show me around? I can only stay a couple of hours before I have to get the bus back to the railway station."

They crossed the bridge.

"What is that grand building over there by the river?"

"It used to be the workhouse. I don't know what it's used for now."

"And where is your house?"

"Behind us, up there on the hill." Kurt pointed.

"I don't know if I'll have time to go up and meet Miss Althorpe."

"She doesn't like visitors anyway."

"But is she treating you well?"

"Yeah."

His mother continued to be enthralled by the location.

"I do like all the stone that they've used for these buildings. It's a reddish colour, very unusual. And oh, look. A little stream running in front of those cottages and right under the road."

"I know, mum. I live here. It's the stream from the mill."

"Where can we sit down and have a drink?"

"We could go to the Lion Hotel at the top of the street by the church."

"Have you made lots of friends?" asked his mother as she drank her cup of tea in the hotel lounge.

"Some. Can you stop asking so many questions."

"Well, I wouldn't have to if you wrote more often." She changed the subject. "I expect Dulverton will be as pretty as a picture at Christmas."

"Perhaps. But I'll be coming home for Christmas, won't I?"

"I wish you were but it's still too dangerous. There are air raids almost every single night."

"We can sleep in the Underground."

"I'm afraid our house got hit the other week. There's nothing left of it, nor the houses either side. You'd have nowhere to come back to."

"Where are you living then?"

"Remember Bill, the man who dug up the backyard for us? He's let me stay at his place. He's got a spare room."

Observing her son's dejected look, Audrey Ziegler sought to cheer him up.

"I saw a fish and chip shop coming up here. Why don't I treat you to some."

It was good to eat something other than eggs and school meals which had gone from mediocre to decidedly unappetising. Potatoes had assumed a particularly large part of the ingredients. There were now dishes such as potato pie, which was a pie without any meat, and potato macaroni without any cheese, and even potatoes for dessert in the guise of a pudding consisting of mashed potatoes insufficiently flavoured with a tiny amount of sugar.

Kurt enjoyed the warmth coming through the newspaper in which the fish and chips were wrapped. Opening it up, he added liberal amounts of salt and vinegar. They ate outside in the street with their fingers. Kurt relished every mouthful.

As he walked back up to the house after waving his mother goodbye, the sky was that soft blue of an autumnal evening, one which promised a cold night to come. The moon had already risen, a pale half globe, and the first star was just visible. The unhappiness which Kurt had experienced at the thought of not going home for Christmas, indeed no longer having a home to go to, had lessened. He had eaten well and was carrying a paper bag full of lemon sherbets, flying saucers, jelly babies, and pear drops, all of which his mother had let him choose from the big glass jars lining the interior wall of the local sweet shop.

Kurt was surprised to see Miss Althorpe in the kitchen waiting for him when he entered. He was perturbed too. Her arms were folded and her face was flushed with anger like a dark grey sky the moment before a thunderstorm. Approaching him without speaking, she slapped him hard on the face causing his head to jolt sideways.

"Ow! What did you do that for?" In shock, Kurt fought to blink back the tears forming.

"I told you to make sure to leave the chicken coop secure. A fox got in last night and killed two of my hens. I don't want you going in there anymore. I'll leave an egg out for you in future. But for the next two weeks you can go without any as punishment. Now get to your room."

Rubbing his cheek, Kurt climbed the stairs. In his bedroom, he slumped onto his bed and sobbed. But it wasn't because Miss Althorpe had hit him. It was because he would be stuck here in this miserable place for Christmas. The temporary comfort brought by today's treats had passed as quickly as the water flowing under Dulverton bridge.

Shortly before the big day, a large parcel arrived with a message written on it that he was not to open it until Christmas Day but Kurt couldn't wait. Ripping off the brown paper, he found warm clothing that his mother had made for him as well as wellington boots for the snow, which she wrote in the accompanying letter she was sure would be coming before long. There was also a Christmas cake in a tin, although Kurt ignored her suggestion that he should share it with Miss Althorpe.

The woman didn't appear to acknowledge the celebration. She hadn't put up any decorations, not unless she had done so in her part of the house. Kurt bought the coloured paper that they sold in the newsagents for making paper chains and strung one on his headboard and put another on the windowsill, yet it didn't feel a bit like Christmas. That was one thing which had been good about his father. Germans seemed to adore this time of year. They'd always had a tree and brightly painted wooden ornaments to decorate it.

On the afternoon of Christmas Eve, he went to the carol service at All Saints Church. It was the first time that he'd gone there, despite Mrs Bishop's invitation to attend when he had first arrived. He wasn't from a religious family, however on that day he needed to feel some connection with the whole reason for Christmas, something to make him feel less alone.

The crenellated tower at the entrance made Kurt believe he was entering a castle. Inside, candles and the arched ceiling of curved beams made it cosy and festive. A man sat playing the organ by the choir stalls from where the choir led the congregation in an enthusiastic singing of carols. Mrs. Bishop beamed when she noticed him and gave him a welcoming wave with the fingers of her right hand.

At the end of the service, Kurt accepted her offer to go to the vicarage. A Christmas tree occupied a large part of the entrance hall. Holly had been hung around the mantelpiece in the drawing room and a fire burned in the grate. There were mince pies to eat and mulled cider to drink. The ambience was warm and convivial. It smelled of good cheer and kindness. Kurt so wished that he could have lived here, but the Bishops already had three evacuees billeted with them.

Returning to Miss Althorpe's was a terrible contrast, a place of chilled silence where joy was always absent. To his surprise, the woman did show some seasonal spirit on Christmas Day, telling him to help himself to the rabbit stew which she had made. Yet even a full stomach couldn't take away the loneliness of that day spent on his own. It had always been the best day of the year. Now it had become the worst. A day to endure, no longer one of smiles and laughter.

CHAPTER 7

Waking the next day to see that there had been an overnight snowfall raised Kurt's mood. The landscape had been transformed from its forlorn and dreary state. In London when it snowed, it never stayed pristine and unsullied once people emerged from their houses and the traffic started. Here there was no one and nothing to disturb it.

Kurt set off through the forest wrapped up against the cold in the scarf, hat, gloves, and thick woolly sweater, all of which his mother had knitted for him. He proceeded along a path set back from the river. The snow must have been several inches deep, and was unmarked save for the occasional paw prints where rabbits and deer had travelled. Kurt grinned as he enthusiastically plunged his wellington boots into the soft snow. With the tree branches above him completely white and bent over so that they touched each other, it was as if he was walking down the aisle of an ice cathedral.

A horse came towards him and he recognised the rider.

"Hello, Kurt, Did you have a good Christmas?"

Barb's smile gave him the collywobbles but in a good way.

"It was quiet."

"Mine too. I've got a sledge back at the farm. Do you fancy having a go?"

Kurt traipsed along behind Bella. He'd never been sledging before, but he'd seen people doing it on Christmas cards and had often wished that he could have a go.

Kurt waited for her outside the farm gate. She came back dragging a roughly hewn home-made wooden sledge behind her. Together they climbed the hill behind the farm. In the valley to their right, they could see the snow topped roofs of Dulverton emitting pencils of smoke which climbed languidly into the sky.

Both of them yelled out with glee as they slid down the slope at an ever increasing speed until the sledge toppled over and they fell off into the powdery white world the ground had become. They got up spitting out snow from their mouths and laughing. Kurt's expression changed to one of concern.

"How did you get that black eye?"

"Oh, that." Barb looked embarrassed, putting her hand up to shield it even though it was too late to hide it. "Bella kicked me. Again?"

"Definitely."

They trudged back up the hill countless times, not stopping until a gruff voice called from the direction of the farm house.

"Barb! What are you up to? Get back here now and get my lunch."

Anxiety seemed to take Barb hostage.

"I'm coming," she shouted. "I must go, we could do it tomorrow if you like."

She ran off with the sledge swaying wildly from side to side as she pulled it behind her.

Kurt was there bright and early. He waited a long time but still she didn't come so he walked towards the farmhouse. The place looked almost abandoned. Little of the paint remained on the front door or window frames. One pane of glass was cracked and another window had been boarded up.

From around the side of the barn a dog that didn't look well fed appeared and began barking, its lips pulled back over its teeth. While Kurt contemplated whether to retreat, the front door to the farmhouse flew open.

"What do you want?" The man wore braces over his undershirt. His face was unshaven and creased with lines of annoyance.

"I've come to see Barb. We were going sledging."

"She's busy." Kurt hesitated. "Be off with you. And don't come round bothering us no more."

As he waded back through the snow, Kurt concluded that he was probably luckier to be without a father. At least he was free to do what he wanted. There was nobody to boss him around any longer.

When school resumed, he waited by the school gates for Barb to arrive. She gave him a smile as weak as milky tea.

"I'm sorry about the other day."

"Your father doesn't seem too friendly."

"I think it's hard for him since mum died. That's the bell, we better get in."

Barb seemed to avoid Kurt after that.

His mother came to visit him again in March, and then in July. It was a hot day and so they sat outside at the Bridge Inn. Being only a minor, Kurt had never been allowed inside a pub. He had often wondered what went on in one that meant children weren't permitted to enter. However, today he had something much more pressing on his mind.

"Everyone at school is saying the Blitz has come to an end. That there's been no bombing since the beginning of May. And now that Hitler's invaded Russia, he needs all his bombers for the Eastern front so the bombing of London won't be starting up again any time soon."

"Yes, it's been such a relief. No more nights spent in the Anderson shelter in Bill's garden. It's so cramped and uncomfortable. At last, I can get a decent night's sleep."

"I want to come home, mum. It'll be safe now. We could find a place for the two of us. I don't care what it's like or how small it is. I can sleep on a sofa. The floor if I have to."

His mother looked down and pushed her glass around in tiny circles on the wooden table, preparing herself for what she must say.

"I've something to tell you, Kurt. Bill and I...we got married."

"Married? But you're still married to dad."

"I was able to divorce him because he deserted us. I know it must be quite a surprise for you."

It was but Kurt had already processed the news and could see that it solved his problem.

"Well, now he'll have a spare room for me so there's nothing stopping me from coming back."

"In a little while. You see, Bill's never had children. We just need to give him a bit of time to get used to the idea."

"But he knows you've got me. Anyway, why would you have married someone who didn't want me?"

"It's more complicated than that. When you grow up, you'll understand."

"Understand? You're just like dad. You don't care about me!"

"Of course I do."

Kurt had already got up and was running across the bridge, ignoring his mother's calls to come back. He ran off into the woods by the river. His dad leaving had been a shock but this was a bigger one.

CHAPTER 8

Kurt didn't stop running until he saw someone standing in the river with a fishing rod, which brought him to an abrupt halt. He went to go back the way that he had come but he'd already been spotted.

"Are you all right?"

It was Barb.

"Yeah."

"You look a little upset." Kurt didn't respond. "I thought you might already have left like the evacuees who came down from Bristol."

"No, not yet." Kurt was feeling too raw to give any further explanation.

"Did you want to have a go at fishing? I've already caught one trout."

Kurt took off his shoes and socks, joining her in the shallow water. The refreshing coolness of it between his toes helped soothe him a little. Barbara demonstrated how to throw the line. Kurt was delighted when he reeled in another fish. It was just the tonic he needed.

"I was going to make a fire and cook them if you'd

like to stay."

Kurt couldn't help but be impressed by her skills; fishing and now starting a fire. She stuck the fish on thin sticks.

"Take this one and hold it near enough the fire to cook but not so close that it gets burned."

They ate with their fingers, licking off every last bit. Kurt couldn't recall when he had eaten anything which had tasted quite so delicious. Afterwards, they remained on the river bank soaking in the bliss of summer while they watched a kingfisher with its blue wings and orange stomach chase insects visible in the shafts of sunlight coming through the gaps between the trees.

"Look over there," whispered Barbara. "There's an otter family coming downstream."

The mother and her two cubs climbed out onto the bank on the opposite side of the river. Their wet fur looked as if it had been slicked back with the grease men used on their hair. The animals spent a brief moment resting before silently sliding back into the water and heading off. Kurt's day had improved considerably. Maybe staying in Dulverton wouldn't be quite so terrible after all.

Barb and Kurt saw each other several times that summer. Always early, he became nervous waiting for her to arrive. There was no denying it, he was infatuated. With her curly chestnut hair, freckled cheeks and large, round face, he thought Barb was the most beautiful girl that he'd ever laid eyes upon. When they weren't together, he found himself thinking about her most of the time.

One day as they walked back along the river from Exebridge, he plucked up courage and slipped his hand into hers. Immediately, she dropped his hand and pulled away. It wasn't the reaction that Kurt had been hoping for.

"Sorry. I didn't mean to-"

"It's not your fault."

They completed their walk in silence. This time when they parted, they made no arrangements to meet up again.

"I'll see you at school when it starts in a couple of weeks," said Barb. She hurried away down the forest path, not once looking back to wave as she normally did.

Infuriated with himself, Kurt kicked a tree trunk after she'd gone. If only he had left well alone. Now he'd gone and spoiled it all. Lost his friend, his only friend. He would just have to try and patch things up when school started.

His heart was beating fast when he entered the school gates on the first day back. Kurt scanned the playground for Barb, but he couldn't see her. The next day with still no sign of her, he approached one of the girls who he'd seen her hanging around with last year.

"Barb's left. She's not coming back."

"Left?"

"Yes, are you deaf?"

The girl glared at him before turning her back on him to talk to her friends.

A couple of times after school Kurt climbed the hill above the farm and sat watching, waiting for the door to open. However, he never saw any sign of Barb.

He thought about running away but Kurt didn't know where he could go. There didn't seem any point trying to get back to London. Instead, he found a job delivering newspapers before school. That would at least ensure that he never ran out of money to buy sweets. They were a big source of comfort to him. Yet even that pleasure was soon denied when the rationing of confectionery was introduced. Worse still ice creams disappeared, the government decreeing that they had no nutritional value.

Kurt loathed this stupid war. From what he could glean reading the papers which he pushed through letter boxes, there seemed no prospect of it ending any time soon. Kurt was thoroughly fed up. He was bored. The days came and went, his tedious daily routine always the same. How he wished that something in his life would change. He craved excitement and adventure, but that seemed most unlikely in this stifling environment. The hills around the town had become walls once more, making him feel trapped. It frustrated him not knowing how much longer he would be stuck here, no end in sight. He was tired of waiting for his life to start.

Getting back to the house from school one afternoon, Kurt drank some milk and munched on a piece of stale bread in the kitchen. The rest of the day stretched out before him, empty and pointless. Her car was here. He'd have to retreat to his room while the hours until bedtime passed by at a snail's pace. At least Kurt had got a new book from school, 'War of the Worlds'. It sounded good.

As he walked along the corridor to go upstairs, Kurt heard something which stopped him in his tracks. The heavy silence of the house was broken by an unfamiliar sound. Somebody was groaning in pain.

It couldn't be Miss Althorpe as she was admonishing the person.

"Shush. You can't make a noise. The boy might hear you. Bite on this cloth."

The hairs on the back of Kurt's neck stood up like a hedgehogs' spiky fur. Something strange, sinister even, was going on beyond that door in the corridor. She never had visitors. Who could it possibly be? Kurt didn't move, straining to hear more.

"Stay there while I go to the kitchen to clean up."

Realising that the door would soon open, Kurt hurried up the stairs as fast as he could without making a sound but it wasn't quickly enough.

"Have you been listening?" Miss Althorpe's tone was frostier than ice.

"No. Listening to what?"

A rabbit in headlights, he was paralysed by the sight of her. She was wearing an apron. It was stained. Stained red.

"Don't lie to me, boy." She slipped her hand into the pocket of her skirt. "Come down. Now."

She pointed a gun at him. In fright, Kurt dropped his book. It clattered down the few stairs between them. Kurt followed.

"I won't ever say anything. Please."

"Shut up and get in there." Miss Althorpe pushed him roughly in the back and through the open door in the corridor and into the dining room.

A man was seated on a dining chair. He looked wild. His hair was untidy, his eyes a mixture of defiance and pain. His clothes were splattered with mud as though he had been walking across fields to avoid roads. A bandage with a crimson patch underneath it was wrapped around his bare arm. His shirt sleeve below the elbow had been cut away.

"Is this him, the boy?"

"Yes, he was spying on us."

"You need to kill him."

The accent was familiar. It was the same as his father's.

CHAPTER 9

"That's easy for you to say," retorted Miss Althorpe. "You'll be out of here and safe on a submarine later tonight. I won't. Where am I going to dispose of a body? If the police find him, I'll hang."

Kurt put his hands out, placing them on the back of one of the dining chairs for support. His legs had turned to paper. He wanted to run, run and not stop, yet Miss Althorpe was right behind him armed with her pistol.

"What do you suggest then?" The sarcastic arrogance in the man's voice cut like a knife.

"You can take him with you."

"Take him with me?"

"Yes, take him with you. His name's Kurt Ziegler, his father's German. You can have him back."

"That's not possible."

"Do you want me to drive you to the coast tonight or not?" The man didn't respond. "Well?"

He breathed out like a bull preparing to charge, but it proved to be all for show.

"All right. You leave me no choice."

"Sit down," she commanded Kurt. Rummaging in

the drawers of the dresser, she found what she wanted and tied his hands to the back of the chair with some string which she pulled so tightly that it cut into his wrists. "Don't try anything stupid. If you do exactly what you're told, you won't come to any harm. And you might get to see your father again. You did say he lived in Germany. Now wouldn't that be nice."

She addressed the man. "You can go to the lounge. You'll be more comfortable there. We don't need to leave until after midnight. You'll be safer here than waiting around on the beach. The boy's not going anywhere. I'll make you something to eat."

Darkness arrived and Kurt was left in it. A three quarter moon visible through the window cast eerie shadows which fell upon the boy like a shroud. Kurt understood that he must get out of here somehow. If she wasn't going to kill him, what's to say that the man wouldn't once they were at sea. And even if he didn't, the last place in the world where he wanted to go was Germany. The prospect terrified him.

This was all his parents' fault. If his father hadn't abandoned them and if his mother hadn't married Bill, he wouldn't be in this situation. He would have been back in London by now, safe, not be here facing kidnapping and possibly death.

And Miss Althorpe, why on earth was she helping a German to escape? She was an unpleasant character, but Kurt had never imagined for one minute that she would be a traitor. He felt like an animal caught in a trap, helpless and knowing that it was only a matter of time until the hunter returned to complete the job.

After a while, his backside became numb from sitting in the chair for too long. He wriggled, trying to move it. A light came on in his mind. Although he was tied to the chair he could stand up, leaning forward with the chair against his back. As quietly as he could manage, Kurt went to the corner of the dining room table and turned around. He tried catching the string on it to see if he could loosen his rope handcuffs. After several attempts, they did. With fumbling fingers, Kurt began fiddling with the knot.

He was as good as blind, unable to see what he was doing. The knot seemed to tighten once more and the sweat of fear made his hands clumsy. Again and again he tried, desperate in the knowledge that at any moment Miss Althorpe would march in, sealing his fate. Finally, the string began to unravel.

His heart in his mouth, Kurt crept towards the kitchen door. Turning the handle as carefully as if he were trying to defuse an unexploded bomb, he opened it and tore down the hill. The police station would be closed, so Kurt decided to head across town to the vicarage to wake Mrs Bishop. She would know where the local policeman lived and he could summon reinforcements to apprehend the traitor and the German.

Kurt's body was electrified. He had gone from

despair and fear to exhilaration and triumph. He jumped in the air, punching it with a fistful of freedom. Kurt would be a national hero, front page news. The other kids at school would change their opinion of him. Everyone would want to be his friend after this. Surely he'd get a medal, presented by the King himself at Buckingham Palace. How could his mother not have him back then. And that tyrant who he currently lived with would be locked up or shot exactly as she deserved to be.

The street was deserted, the road a shiny black from recent rainfall. The Bridge Inn had long since closed. The drinkers would all be snoring in their beds, blissfully unaware of what was going on tonight in their little town. As he ran up the high street, his footsteps resounding off the pavement, he heard an unwelcome noise, the noise of a car. A quick look confirmed that it was hers. Kurt had reached the top of the high street. To get to the vicarage, he had to go right and then left up the road for some distance. That was no good. They would catch up with him. Instead, Kurt went straight on towards the church where the road which led to it came to an end. He could probably cut through that way.

As he sprinted up the church path, Kurt glanced behind him. The two of them were out of the vehicle, racing in his direction. Going around the back of the church, he couldn't see a way out. The graveyard rose in narrow grassed terraces. The surrounding wall appeared to contain no exit. Their footsteps were getting ever closer. The exhilaration which had propelled him was seeping fast, leaving him drained and desperate. He must hide. His life depended on it.

Crouching behind one of the numerous headstones, he waited. Putting his hand out to steady himself, he drew quickly back. The old stone, damp and slimy, was like touching death itself.

"I think he must have got out. Why don't you head off that way, and I'll go around to the front in case he doubled-back."

Kurt heard the man walk away. Looking out from his hiding place, Kurt could discern the spindly outline of Miss Althorpe gradually also moving away but still too close for him to leave and not be noticed. He needed to be patient, she'd soon be gone. Then he could emerge and continue on his way to the safety of the vicarage, his nightmare over.

"Ha!" A vice of clammy fingers enveloped his neck and a barrel of metal pressed into the small of his back. The man had outwitted him. Kurt was steered towards the car and pushed roughly into the boot. The man slammed it shut.

"Don't make a peep if you want to live." The man didn't sound as if he cared one way or the other.

CHAPTER 10

The journey lasted an eternity, or so it seemed to Kurt in his confined space. At some point he must have fallen asleep because the next thing he remembered was being told to get out. Miss Althorpe remained in the car.

"Good luck," she said to the German through the open window.

"Thank you. You will be rewarded for your efforts when Germany wins this war."

"Cheer up, Kurt. No need to look so glum." There wasn't a trace of empathy in her voice. She moved the corners of her lips to produce a miserly smile.

Kurt had no idea where he was. From what he could make out, they must be somewhere by the coast. A black ribbon of river ran below to the left of them, yet he could hear the swish and swoosh of waves on pebbles. It was something which would once have reminded him of a carefree summer's day trip but now it spoke only of impending doom. They walked along a path. Below them, he could make out small boats bobbing about. The man pulled on one of the ropes tethering them.

"Climb down that ladder." They got into a rowing boat. The man took hold of the oars. "Scheisse!" The man shouted from the pain of his wounded arm as he began rowing.

Soon they had left the estuary and were out at sea. Kurt had never been on the ocean before. He gripped the sides of the boat as it rose and dropped over the waves. Unable to swim, he was petrified of drowning. The man took a torch from the bag draped across his shoulder and flashed it on and off several times. Farther out, someone flashed back. The man quickened his strokes.

They came alongside a long, black shape floating on the surface like a motionless whale. Men standing on it reached out their arms and helped them climb on.

"We need to get going," said one.

They climbed the ladder up the conning tower and descended the interior one into the submarine. Darkness became light, yet it was an entirely different world to one that Kurt had ever inhabited. A claustrophobic, windowless tube of dials and pipes. A miasma of body odour and mould caused his nose to wrinkle in protest.

"I'm the captain. You must be a very important person," said a man to Kurt's captor. "My men weren't too pleased when we got orders to divert. We've been out in the Atlantic for three months, and they're very keen to be back in Saint Nazaire and finally off this boat."

"I'm grateful. I have some extremely useful

intelligence for the war effort."

"Who's this you've brought along? He looks a bit young to be a spy."

"He discovered me in a safe house. It was too risky to leave him behind. The boy's half German."

"Do you speak German, lad?" Relieved that he hadn't been killed, Kurt was still afraid and struggling to take in all that had happened. He could only manage a nod in reply. "You can sleep on a bunk if you can find a spare one. We'll be back at base in about twenty hours."

Kurt wandered along the narrow walkway which wasn't wide enough to pass another without both turning sideways. It began to slope downwards as the craft dived. Alarmed, he put his hands out to stabilise himself. Where space wasn't filled with equipment, there were narrow strips to sleep, laid out like bunk beds except for certain areas which only had a place to lie down on one level above or below some piece of kit. Kurt couldn't yet see any beds which weren't occupied. When he found a place which was available it was beneath what he assumed from its design must be a torpedo. He slid in cautiously, worried that he might set the weapon off were he to knock it.

Kurt wished that he was back in his dull but predictable life. The constant creaking of the hull from the pressure of the ocean outside scared him. Being in here was as if he'd been buried alive in a steel coffin. He imagined the hull cracking, water gushing in and engulfing him. Cold, salty liquid that would make him splutter and choke as it filled his lungs and nostrils while he flailed around in a vain attempt to fight off the inevitability of death. He wanted to cry out for help but nobody other than his captors would hear him.

The sound of German voices, harsh and angry to his ears, was a deeply unsettling experience. A confirmation that he was already beyond escape or rescue. On edge and sleeping little, Kurt stayed put for almost the entire journey. He didn't want to draw attention to himself, and there was really nowhere else to go. However, it wasn't possible to be invisible in the confined quarters of a submarine. Men were walking past him the whole time. They were curious but not unfriendly. Each sported a thick beard and their clothes were grimy. He hadn't expected the German military to look so unkempt.

The reality was that because of limited capacity, the water carried on board could only be used for drinking. The men could neither shave nor wash, even though they were out on patrol for months at a time. A man with remnants of his last meal in his beard brought him some food in a tin bowl which Kurt wolfed down, despite that from its taste it appeared to have absorbed the ever present smell of diesel oil. The man offered some advice.

"When you grow up, don't join us. Choose to serve on a boat, a plane, a tank, anything but a submarine. Being on this thing so long doesn't just make you stink, it messes with your mind."

An awful realisation punched Kurt hard in the gut. In the space of only one day, his life had changed forever. He would grow up inside the Reich, and have to fight for them. With luck, he would soon be out of here, but he would still be trapped no matter where in Germany they sent him, unable to return home. He wondered if they would know where his father was and if he would be sent to live with him. At least it would be someone he knew, someone who might care about what happened to him. It was a branch of hope to cling to.

Once the French coast was in view, the submarine surfaced. The diesel engines were turned on, allowing speed to increase. The men were permitted to smoke and lit up, some with their hands shaking like drug addicts who couldn't wait for their next shot. It was one of the few pleasures intermittently allowed them. Soon, the vessel had filled with a thick smog which made Kurt cough.

As they entered the harbour, Kurt went outside with others to watch. It was good to emerge from that windowless tube into the bracing sea air and feel alive again. The men were in high spirits. They had lived and survived another mission. There was the prospect of a trip home for some. Others might have only dry land and a brothel to look forward to, but that seemed heaven after what they had endured. Kurt was the only one who was fearful of what today would bring. Approaching what looked like giant concrete garages without doors, the submarine docked inside one of them.

"Follow me," said Kurt's kidnapper as they disembarked. He marched him to a small building in the large yard beyond the submarine pens. Telling Kurt to wait outside, he went in. Kurt could hear the conversation through the open window. Although he hadn't practised his German for nearly two years, he hadn't forgotten it.

"There's a boy outside who came over from England with me. Kurt Ziegler's his name. Says his father, Otto, moved back to Germany shortly before the war started. Doesn't know where but says the man lived in Düsseldorf before moving to England. Can you get someone to call the Gauleiter's office there and see if they can trace his father so that the boy can be sent to him."

"And if not?"

"Not my problem. I have to leave for Berlin straightaway."

The door opened and Kurt jumped away from the window.

"You can go and sit on that bench over there. Wait until someone tells you what to do."

The man departed without a further word. Kurt watched him go, his coat billowing in the strong breeze like some evil count from a children's story. Kurt didn't know his name and never would. The man who had been the cause of his exile would forever remain anonymous to him.

Kurt sat for a long time. Military personnel passed by but no one spoke to him. He was beginning to wish that he was back on the submarine. Out here in the open, he worried that he would be forgotten about.

"Kurt Ziegler." The man in front of him appeared no more friendly than the spy had been. "Here is a travel pass. Go to the station. You can see it from here, beyond the railings. There's a train leaving for Paris in thirty minutes. When you arrive, speak to a soldier and show him these papers."

"Am I going to my father's?"

"I expect so."

The man left before Kurt could ask any more questions.

He remained where he was, quite overwhelmed by events. Kurt had travelled by himself from London to Dulverton, however this was an altogether much more challenging experience. Examining the papers which had been given to him, he read that he was the son of Otto Ziegler and that he was to be afforded free passage to somewhere Kurt hadn't heard of and had no clue of where it might be. It wasn't where his father came from. Perhaps it was where he was living now.

A few minutes later, the soldier returned.

"What are you still doing here? Miss the train and you'll be thrown off the base and have to fend for yourself. Now move it."

CHAPTER 11

On the train, Kurt sat opposite an elderly French couple. The woman smiled at him, displaying crooked yellow teeth.

"Tu vas à Paris?" *(Are you going to Paris?)*

Kurt had paid enough attention in French lessons at school to understand and nodded before looking out of the window to avoid further questions. If he said that he was English, how would he explain what he was doing here, and he didn't want to say that he was German. He couldn't imagine that the French would have taken kindly to being invaded.

However, he couldn't help himself when the woman took a baguette and some cheese out of her shopping bag. The aroma of the fresh bread was irresistible and his hungry eyes betrayed him.

"Tu as faim?" *(Are you hungry?)*

Gratefully Kurt accepted the hunk of bread which she broke off and handed to him. He was less certain about the cheese which she offered. It assaulted his nostrils, a smell of sweaty old socks which reminded him of the interior of the submarine. Cautiously, he nibbled a small piece and was surprised to find that it tasted delicious and had a lovely creamy texture.

"Camembert," said the woman.

His worries about conversation were resolved when the couple got off at the next stop. It was already night when the train arrived in Paris. The soldier to whom he showed his travel papers called out to another. Put on a military vehicle, Kurt was driven at speed across the city. Arriving at another station, he was taken to a train. It appeared to be a freight train, cattle wagons by the look of them. There must have been over twenty. It was a long walk to the only passenger carriage at the front next to the engine where Kurt had been instructed to board. Several soldiers stood on the platform chatting. Some held guard dogs who barked almost constantly, pulling on their leads as though they had found something. Kurt went inside and sat by a window. As the engine began puffing out smoke as dirty as a London smog, the men climbed aboard with the dogs in tow.

"You should get some sleep," said one of them, observing Kurt's anxious look. "We've a long journey ahead of us."

The early morning sun shining directly in his face woke Kurt. Their train had halted in the countryside. He was the only one remaining in the carriage. The soldiers were outside smoking. Kurt decided to stretch his legs too. They ached from having to sit upright all night.

"You. Stay on the train," called out one of the guards as Kurt appeared at the open door.

Kurt retreated. He thought he heard voices coming from the freight wagons. But that couldn't be right, a lack of sleep must be playing tricks on his mind. The soldiers got back on and offered him some of their food.

"Are we in Germany yet?" His voice squeaked involuntarily.

"Yes," came a reply without offering any further information. All that day they travelled. Kurt thought the country looked pleasant enough but it was still intimidating to him. This was Nazi Germany, a war machine hell bent on subjugating the entire continent. As they passed through towns, he tried to catch the names of the stations, although they didn't mean anything to him. The only two places in Germany that he had heard of were Düsseldorf and Berlin.

It proved to be a much bigger country than England. They were still going come nightfall. Even by the next morning, they hadn't reached their destination. This part of Germany looked much poorer. The houses weren't well maintained, and paved roads had largely given way to dirt tracks. With a huge sigh of smoke and a grating squeal of brakes, the train came to a standstill.

"This is where you get off."

They had halted in the middle of nowhere or so it appeared to Kurt. All he could see through the window were fields.

"Where am I supposed to go?"

"Walk down the road for a few kilometres. You'll see a monastery. You can't miss it."

"A monastery?"

"Yes, a monastery. You can be a monk." The other soldiers laughed.

Kurt stepped off the train into an unknown world, afraid and wishing his mother was there to protect him. He stood watching the train depart. It had been a place of temporary safety. It trundled towards ugly looking brick buildings surrounded by barbed wire fences and watch towers. However, Kurt was too concerned about his own situation to speculate what or who might be kept there. His thoughts were focused on what was going to happen to him. How could it possibly be that he was being sent to a monastery? The prospect sounded even less appealing than living at Miss Althorpe's. He didn't understand why he hadn't been sent to join his father.

Kurt began walking down the poorly surfaced road pockmarked with potholes. He had no choice. There was nothing else that he could do, abandoned and alone deep in the heart of the Reich.

Rounding a bend he saw it, standing proud above the flat farmland that stretched to the horizon. A long stone building painted white with an ochre tiled roof. A church and its tall spire dominated one end, a turret the other. When he got closer, Kurt was enchanted to see a stork take flight from the roof of the building and head in his direction. Its enormous wings looked like those of an aircraft as the bird flew across the sky just above him. The rush of wind it created brushed his face as he gazed upwards. Maybe it was a good omen.

Drawn towards substantial wooden doors which were open, he entered the large rectangular space constituting an interior courtyard. There were no monks to be seen. Kurt wondered which of the many doors he should go knock on, grinding his shoes into the gravel as he prevaricated.

He didn't have to decide. A young man in uniform came through one of them and marched briskly over to him. The man was taller than Kurt with wavy blonde hair. He appeared extremely sure of himself as if life had always gone his way and smelled strongly of cologne.

"Heil Hitler." His arm leapt into the air like that of a puppet on a string. "Are you Ziegler? Kurt Ziegler?"

"Yes."

"Yes, sir!"

"Yes, sir," repeated Kurt.

"That's better. We're glad to have you. Your father's a hero. I'm Stammführer Hofmann."

A hero? That was a word Kurt had never associated with his father. He couldn't imagine what the man could possibly have done to deserve such a status.

"You are in one of the camps that the Führer has set up for children of the Reich to protect them from the enemy criminals who are bombing our cities. Here you will be safe and learn how to serve the Führer, and be ready to fight and die for our glorious Fatherland if necessary when you are older. I am in command here. I will show you to your dormitory where you will change into your uniform. I will then escort you to your classroom where I will introduce you to your teacher and your classmates."

The room to which Hofmann escorted Kurt was no bigger than a cell into which two wooden bunk beds had been squeezed with a space between them no wider than the walkway on the submarine. Hofmann left Kurt to change, saying that he'd be back to collect him in five minutes.

Kurt concluded that a monk must once have inhabited the room. The single window was a tiny square up high and barely let in any light. The room was more like a prison than a bedroom. The stone walls were cold and damp to the touch like the gravestone in Dulverton had been. It was as if death was still stalking him, unhappy that it hadn't yet succeeded in claiming him.

He sat down on one of the beds, still trying to come to terms with all that had transpired. However, there was little time to dwell on that. This already felt like an environment which would be much more threatening than being the odd one out at the local school in a small English town. He needed to avoid becoming a victim if he was to survive here. How much and for how long his father being a hero might protect him he didn't know.

The uniform had been laid out neatly like priestly

garments. Kurt took off his clothes and put on the black shorts and tan shirt with a Nazi armband He wasn't sure what he was supposed to do with the remaining black cloth and a brown toggle.

"Why don't you have your neckerchief on?" demanded Hofmann when he returned.

"I'm sorry, sir. I'm not familiar with how it should be worn."

"I will show you just this once." He put the black cloth around Kurt's neck as if it were a loosely fitting tie with the toggle holding it in place. "Now, Ziegler." He leaned forward, his eyes burrowing into Kurt. "It is important if you wish to fit in and prosper that you give a positive impression of how you came to be here. Let me explain."

CHAPTER 12

Marched down a long corridor, Kurt was led out into the courtyard and into the church. It was a place of worship no more, or at least of Christian worship. Whatever furniture it may once have contained had been replaced by large tables behind which sat boys on long benches.

Seeing who was escorting Kurt, they immediately jumped to their feet, shouting "Heil Hitler" in unison as did the man standing at the front where once the altar would have been. All religious iconography had gone. Draped over the main window was a huge Nazi flag, and a large framed photograph of the Führer had taken the place of Jesus. There was a new, compulsory religion now.

"Ziegler, this is your teacher, Herr Schneider." Kurt shook the hand offered by a bald man. He was shorter than Kurt, yet his face conveyed a steely determination to dominate his pupils. "Class, you may sit back down. This is Kurt Ziegler, son of Obersturmführer Otto Ziegler, a hero of the fatherland who has been awarded the Iron Cross for outstanding bravery on the Russian front.

Ziegler comes to us from England so you must give him some leeway while he learns our ways."

There was a murmuring of disapproval as the word 'England' was repeated amongst the boys.

"Quiet! I didn't ask you to comment. Ziegler, why don't you tell us how you came to be here."

All eyes turned on him in eager expectation. Kurt breathed in deeply. This was his chance, his one chance to avoid making his life what would probably otherwise be a living hell.

"I was born and brought up in London."

"Louder!" demanded Hofmann.

"I was born and brought up in London. My mother is English. Before the war began, my father returned to Germany to serve the Reich. I wanted to come too but my mother told the authorities and I was sent away into the country. Despite that, I never gave up the dream of escaping. I ran away more than once but they tracked me down and punished me. Finally, I was successful. I got to the coast and stole a small boat and made my way across the Channel. Now I am able to do my duty."

Rapturous applause led by the two adults followed his speech. Kurt was relieved it was over, and that he had remembered what Hofmann had instructed him to say.

"Ziegler here is an inspiration, an example to us all. Herr Schneider, I shall leave you to continue with your class."

Kurt couldn't help but smile as he went to sit with the other boys, many of whom wanted to shake his hand. It seemed for once that he wouldn't be the outsider.

Three lads of a similar age shared his tiny room. There was Klaus Becker and Jürgen Meier. Athletic looking specimens and arrogant like Hofmann, they were nonetheless cautious around Kurt, no doubt because of the almost mythical status bestowed upon him.

"Tell us more about how you crossed the English Channel," insisted Klaus the first night.

Kurt found himself enjoying the attention as he fabricated a tale of daring. One that he would get to repeat many times over the days to come.

The third boy didn't have the confidence of Klaus and Jürgen. Quiet and shy, Dieter Schmidt melted into the background. He wasn't your typical Hitler Jugend, or Hitler Youth, material. Overweight, with stubby fingers and cheeks in which air seemed to be permanently trapped, his voice hadn't yet broken or if it had, it remained unusually high. Most of the time he had the look of a frightened animal. Dieter was an easy object of derision, and Klaus and Jürgen ribbed him mercilessly.

"Just as well you didn't have Schmidt in your boat. With his weight, he would have sunk it before you even got out of the harbour."

Kurt joined in the laughter. It was a novelty to be part of the 'in crowd' and he liked it.

Kurt's days quickly settled into the government

imposed routine. Woken at six, the boys were marched outside to participate in the raising of the Nazi flag. Total silence was required unless those in charge said otherwise. After breakfast, class began. For much of the time the children were merely indoctrinated with Nazi dogma which the boys had to learn by heart. Teachers didn't seek thoughts or analysis. Obedience was expected, not opinions.

This wasn't the sometimes bumbling, slightly chaotic but generally well-meaning approach to evacuation practised in England. Children weren't placed in private homes with families and integrated into a local community. Relocation to a Kinderlandverschickung (Child Land Dispatch), or KLV, was compulsory, and an essential part of the state's programme to produce a fanaticised youth to grow into Hitler's fighting machine. Untainted by being able to recall a time before the Third Reich, they would be reliable and have unquestioning faith in the regime.

Kurt had no choice but to join in the ritual denunciation of Jews and other "Untermensch", or sub-humans, such as people of Slavic or Romany origin. The difference between him and the other boys was that Kurt didn't believe what they were told, albeit he was obliged to keep such thoughts to himself. Dissent of any kind wasn't tolerated. It wasn't too long before Kurt began to question whether being popular in such a place was a good thing. His fantasy of becoming a hero had become true but not in the way he had imagined.

Afternoons were devoted to physical activity. But it didn't involve running around kicking a ball as in soccer, or a game of cricket played in brilliant whites on a village green like in England. Here, it was all about preparing for battle. They were taught how to handle weapons and marched off to assault courses. As they crawled under barbed wire through a muddy morass, live ammunition was fired above them, and grenades exploded nearby.

Returning to his room one afternoon, Kurt caught Jürgen in the act of tearing up a photograph and scattering the pieces on Dieter's bed.

"What are you doing?"

"What does it look like I'm doing? Schmidt's a mummy's boy. He's been keeping a photo of his mother under his pillow. He's such a baby."

Kurt didn't attempt to stop Jürgen. When Dieter arrived back, he quickly gathered the torn shreds and placed them back under his pillow before lying on his side and facing the wall. Jürgen and Klaus gave each other the thumbs up and grinned.

Kurt found out that they weren't actually in Germany at all, but in occupied Poland. When Kurt asked what had happened to the monks who had resided here before them, Klaus pulled his index finger sharply across his neck and smirked with approval.

One morning, Kurt was called out of class by Hofmann and marched outside. Hofmann gave no explanation, which made Kurt nervous. Had something happened? Was the charade over, his usefulness to the authorities at an end?

Two cars drove into the courtyard, raising a cloud of dust as they did so. From out of one stepped two men. One held a camera, the other a pen and notepad. From the other car emerged the driver who opened the door for his passenger, a man in a black military uniform which Kurt recognised from lessons as that of the Schutzstaffel, the SS. It was worn by a man who Kurt hadn't seen for a considerable time.

"Heil Hitler," said his father. Kurt understood how he should respond. The photographer clicked his camera and smiled. He had the money shot. Father and son, both heroes of the Reich, giving the Nazi salute.

"Obersturmführer Ziegler," asked the journalist. "What do you think of what your son did?"

Kurt tried not to shudder as his father's arm went around his shoulder.

"I am extremely proud of him. When we lived together in London, I taught him about the glories of National Socialism. We read 'Mein Kampf' together. It was hard for the boy, though. Each day at school, he was fed anti-German propaganda. I am glad that he refused to be browbeaten and courageously crossed the English Channel to be here."

"And Kurt, you must be proud of your father, a hero of the Fatherland."

Again, Kurt knew what was expected.

"Yes, I am."

"Excellent. Now let my colleague take some more photos."

Father and son forced smiles and shook hands until the photographer declared himself satisfied.

"You will be front-page national news," said the journalist. "I shall arrange to have a copy of the newspaper delivered to you. Thank you both, we have everything that we require."

"Good. Well, I must be going too. Goodbye, Kurt," said his father without a smile or a handshake this time.

Dumbfounded, Kurt watched the vehicles leave. Was that it? His father had come all the way from the front just for a photo opportunity, and had nothing to say to his son. Kurt's opinion of the man reached a new low.

CHAPTER 13

That afternoon, Kurt stood in line behind other boys waiting for his turn to run towards a high wooden wall and haul himself up and over it using the rope dangling down from the top. He could see that it would require quite a jump to grab it. Fortunately for Kurt, he was growing into a strapping young man, able to cope with the assault courses without too much difficulty. The sparrow-like legs of his childhood had developed into stocky thighs and strong calf muscles.

Laughter told him someone up ahead must have tried and failed. He leaned his head out to see past those blocking his view. The boy had fallen face down in the mud. Hofmann was screaming at him like a maniac, demanding that the boy get up immediately and do it again.

The boy walked back and made another run at the wall. His limbs didn't coordinate well. When he ran, his legs went out to the side. It was Dieter. Once again, he didn't succeed. And a third time he failed. Hofmann closed his eyes and shook his head with disgust before nodding at a couple of other boys. They left the line and as Dieter got to his knees to stand, they each grabbed an arm and dragged him away backwards and out of sight as if he were a carcass.

Returning later to the dorm, Kurt found Dieter, sitting on his bed still splattered with dirt, his face swollen and dried blood coating the gap between his mouth and his nose.

"What happened?"

"I wasn't able to climb up that high fence. I tried, I tried my best. Some of the other boys set upon me and beat me up."

"Didn't any of those in charge notice?"

"Of course they did. Hofmann gets them to do it. No one does anything without his permission."

"What? He told them to attack you?"

"He doesn't have to say anything. He only has to give the nod. I've seen him do it many times. It's the law of the jungle here. If you fail, you're picked upon. Surely you must have noticed that by now. I wish I could be a hero like you. I'd be safe then, not living each day in perpetual fear."

In Dieter Schmidt, Kurt saw a reflection of himself as he used to be. An outcast, someone whose only crime was that he was different. Kurt experienced a sudden outpouring of sympathy for the boy. He wanted to share the truth with Dieter to make him feel better. Kurt knew what it was like to be ostracised, to be the underdog.

But he couldn't share his secret. Hofmann had made it abundantly clear when Kurt had first arrived that things wouldn't go well for him if he didn't stick strictly to the script of how he had come to be here. Kurt carried a deep loathing for that man. Hofmann was the breath of death, sucking up the oxygen of joy and hope that would normally exist amongst a group of teenagers. Instead, they were taught to admire brutality and hatred, to despise and destroy anyone that didn't meet Nazi norms, and to not regard such people as fellow human beings.

"You should go clean yourself up before the other two get back," was all Kurt said.

A few days later, Kurt received a copy of 'Der Angriff' which was printed in Berlin. There, as promised, on the front page was a picture of Kurt and his father under the headline 'Teenage boy risks life to flee England to fight for the Fatherland'. Although it was all an elaborate hoax, Kurt already understood enough about Nazi Germany to be thankful that they had chosen to make a propaganda hero out of him. He had seen what happened to boys who were deemed failures. Bullying was endemic and encouraged. Only a lie protected Kurt.

Sometimes, in the evenings, the boys got to watch newsreels. Always they portrayed Hitler as leading the nation to victory after glorious victory. Kurt was sceptical. After all, everything they had said about how he had come to be here wasn't true so why wouldn't the other news be false also. And it seemed ages since they'd been told the army was on the outskirts of Moscow and Russia on the verge of collapse, so why was the fighting still going on? America too had recently joined the war, which must surely change things. Yet its intervention was dismissed as irrelevant.

Kurt's suspicions that Germany might no longer be having it all its own way were confirmed when Dieter shared the news which he'd received in a letter from his mother. She told him the army on the eastern front was falling back. His father had written to her saying that he didn't believe Russia could be beaten. Another letter from home not long afterwards described a massive British and American air raid on Dieter's home town of Hamburg, creating a firestorm which had destroyed most of the city. Dieter let Kurt read it. His mother was so thankful, she wrote, that Dieter was safe and out of harm's way.

He got Kurt to promise not to mention what his mother had written, fearing it might get her into trouble. Klaus and Jürgen soaked up all they were fed by the Nazis like sponges, who would regurgitate a puddle of propaganda at the slightest prompting. They would surely show no hesitation in reporting any suspicion of disloyalty.

Kurt wished that he was able to write to his own mother. However, what could he possibly say? The boys' correspondence was routinely monitored to ensure that it didn't contain disloyal statements, and that there were no complaints about conditions at the KLV. Kurt didn't want to write to her saying that he had run away to fight for Germany, and he knew he couldn't risk telling the truth. In bed at night he would think of home, hoping at least to dream of being back there. Yet such dreams as he could remember come morning were traumatic ones all taking place within the hateful confines of this dystopia which he couldn't leave. Kurt yearned for the war to end so that he could go back to England. He missed the soothing hills surrounding Dulverton, being free to wander amongst them, and not having every waking hour controlled and regimented.

Occasionally, he thought of running but he never summoned up the courage to do so. If courage was what it required. It seemed foolhardy to attempt to escape. He told himself that he must learn to be patient. There would surely be an end to this as there was to everything else.

"I can't wait until we are old enough to go to war," complained Klaus. They were all together in their tiny room at the end of the day, Dieter and Jürgen sitting on their beds, Klaus and Kurt standing.

"Knowing my luck, it will all be over before I get the chance," lamented Jürgen.

"I don't see why we have to bother with lessons. We should spend the entire time training to become the best possible soldiers that we can be," said Klaus

"I agree. What about you, Schmidt? Probably not,

eh? You'd shit your pants if you saw the enemy." The two bullies giggled.

"Leave him alone," protested Kurt.

"I don't understand why you protect him, Ziegler. Just what's got into you lately?" Eyes narrowed and fists clenched with aggression, Klaus blocked Kurt against the outside wall of their room. Kurt stood his ground. Another growth spurt had made him the tallest and strongest of the four.

"Let me past."

For a moment Klaus refused to move, a stag about to lock horns with his opponent.

"Lucky for you that you're Hofmann's pet." Klaus relented, restricting himself to a body bump as Kurt went out into the corridor.

Before long, the wish of Jürgen and Klaus that education should end was granted. All pretence at it was abandoned, even if the outcome wasn't entirely what they had been hoping for.

"From tomorrow, instead of lessons you will begin working in the fields. More supplies are required for our heroic fighters at the front. We must play our part by growing our own food," announced their teacher at the start of their last class.

The youths were marched off to different farms. German families had moved into the area, replacing the previous Polish owners whose properties had been confiscated. It was the culmination of the Nazis' vision for the future. All the way to the Urals at the eastern limit of

European Russia, the locals would be dispossessed to create 'Lebensraum' for Germans to repopulate the land. Those of the original inhabitants who weren't required for slave labour could be eliminated by starvation to ensure racial purity.

Kurt was pleased to be outside, even when it rained. School here had only been brainwashing by another name. And they were given good coats to keep out winter's chill. He wasn't aware that they had been ripped from the backs of Jews.

Dieter and he got to work on the same farm. Despite the unremitting drudgery of their existence, seasons came and went with surprising speed. Perhaps it was because each day was the same with nothing of note to make one day stand out from another. Life had become a repetitive blur. There were only a handful of incidents that Kurt remembered and they were ones of cruelty, ones he preferred to try and forget, such as the two adolescents executed following an allegation of engaging in 'unnatural practices', and the young woman with her baby who had come begging for food. Hofmann had despatched them with gunshots.

Kurt reached the age of fifteen, not that birthdays were celebrated. Once he had been excited to be a year older, but no longer. Now it meant that he was a year closer to being conscripted.

Returning to the KLV each day remained like returning to a jail. The exterior eye appeal of the building merely disguised what it was, a place of tyranny over which Hofmann ruled with an iron fist. One that would punch anyone who stepped out of line, including someone who everybody else believed to be a hero. The thought that the war couldn't last for ever was Kurt's one comfort, that one day he would get his freedom, or at least something other than this life.

One evening on getting back from working in the fields, there was unexpected news for Kurt.

"Hofmann wants to see you." There was an undisguised glee in Jürgen's voice.

Kurt didn't expect the man would be offering him coffee and strudel, and racked his brains as he ascended the circular stone staircase to Hofmann's office, desperately trying to think what he may have done or said to warrant an invitation that struck fear into the heart of every resident of the KLV. Kurt believed that he had always been careful to keep his true opinions to himself, and to date that act of self- preservation had served him well.

Located like an eagle's eyrie on the top floor of the tower from where he could survey his prey below, Hofmann's quarters were like his very own Berchtesgaden, an impression cemented by its Nazi paraphernalia. The door was already open. Hofmann was sitting behind his desk. A large photo of Hitler shaking his hand took pride of place on the wall behind him.

"You wanted to see me, Stammführer Hofmann." Kurt's mouth was as dry as dust as he uttered the words.

"Yes, Ziegler. I have received reports questioning your loyalty. That you enjoy the company of weaklings, and that despite all the care which we have lavished upon you, you might still not be reliable." Hofmann stood up and came over to Kurt, not stopping until their faces were almost touching. Kurt wanted to move back but he didn't dare to. "I'm sure I don't need to remind you that I made you, and that I can break you. You are a fake, Ziegler, nothing but a fraud. Here, only you and I know that, but don't imagine that your status as a hero protects you. If you no longer suit my purposes, I can have you dealt with. The myth of Kurt Ziegler, a legend of the Reich, will continue to exist, but you wouldn't. The choice is yours. Dismissed."

Kurt's steps as he descended from the tower were slow and heavy. He had become too complacent about the precariousness of his position. His life hung by a thread and a mad man held the scissors. His suspicions that Klaus and Jürgen were the source of the accusation were confirmed by the unyielding stares of triumph which his adversaries gave him when he returned to the dormitory.

"What happened?" asked Dieter the moment the other two had left the room.

"Becker and Meier have been spreading rumours about me, about my commitment. I can't stand up for you any longer, I'm sorry."

Klaus and Jürgen didn't wait long to test if Kurt had heeded Hofmann's warning. That same evening, they made Dieter crawl along the corridor on all fours and make snorting noises like a pig while others stood at their doors laughing at the spectacle while delivering the occasional kick to hurry him along. Kurt watched and said nothing.

The next day, their humiliation of Dieter reached a new level. They made him run around the courtyard naked as they chased him with birch twigs, caning him each time they caught up with him. Kurt had to stand there and pretend to laugh with the others, although he despised himself for doing so. A quick upwards glance confirmed what he suspected, those eyes were watching. Eyes which kept a close and constant watch, and ears which heard all that went on out of sight of those eyes. Ears which listened eagerly to reports from boys recruited to spy on their companions in this world of dog eat dog. From his elevated position above them, Hofmann viewed the spectacle from his window.

Fortunately, Dieter's tormentors soon got bored with their new games and after that incident left him alone. They could start again whenever they might feel like it, no one was going to stop them. Not long afterwards, however, everybody's attention was captured by something else, something that promised more excitement than picking upon somebody who never retaliated.

"We must all be prepared to defend our homeland to achieve victory regardless of age," pronounced Hofmann at early morning roll call one late September day. "The Bolsheviks are making temporary inroads. But there is no need to be disheartened. New weapons of indescribable power are being developed by our brilliant scientists which will deliver the enemy a knock out blow. Soon they will be ready for operational use. Until then, we must buy time with our unflinching resistance. There is no option but to fight, and fight to the death if we have to. The Russians are barbarians. If they aren't driven back, they will rape your mothers and sisters before murdering them. And should they take you alive, they will torture you in the most brutal fashion before putting you to death or work you like slaves until you die from hunger and exhaustion. So will you join me when we are ordered to go?"

"Yes," roared the assembled adolescents with fire in their eyes, still ignorant of the hellish reality of combat.

"And what should we do to any who refuse, or desert their post?"

"Kill them! Kill them!" chanted the crowd like Romans in a coliseum demanding that the emperor order the losing gladiator to be put to death.

Yet again Kurt had no option but to go along with these lemmings, in the same way that he had been forced to do since the day he arrived. But he realised that he could no longer procrastinate. Hiding from the war and awaiting its end would no longer save him. Out in the fields and unable to be overheard, Kurt shared what he had resolved to do.

"I'm not staying here to be killed fighting the Russians."

Dieter stopped digging and looked at him as if he had lost his sanity.

"But you're a hero of the Reich."

"Can you promise to keep a secret?"

"Yes, I suppose so."

"Swear on your life because mine will be over if you don't keep what I'm about to tell you to yourself."

"I swear."

"That crap about me being a hero is all a lie, more Nazi propaganda. I was kidnapped, brought from England against my will. It suited them to make up the story." Dieter's mouth dropped open. "That's why I don't trust anything Hofmann says. I know they tell us that the British and Americans' invasion of France was a failure, and that they're driving them back into the sea but I don't believe it. I'm going to head west until I reach the front line.

"But they'll execute you if you run."

"Only if they catch me. Why don't you come along?"

"It would be dangerous."

"Dieter, you won't survive otherwise. We can travel at night and hide during the day."

"It's so far."

"Not as far as Siberia. That's where the Russians will send you if they don't shoot you. And they'd work you until you dropped down dead like Hofmann said. At least with my way, when the war is over you'll have a real chance of getting back home."

"I'm scared to run."

"So am I, but I'm more frightened of what will happen if I remain."

"When would you leave?"

"Tonight. There's no point waiting. They could send us off to fight any day now."

"How will you know which way to go?"

"I copied the map in the classroom onto a piece of paper which I've hidden under my pillow."

Dieter didn't ask any more questions and went back to digging as though ignoring the issue might make it go away.

CHAPTER 14

After work, they walked back in silence. Kurt hoped that he hadn't made a mistake sharing the truth with Dieter. He might tell Jürgen and Klaus if they beat him up, demanding he confess any unpatriotic thoughts Kurt had shared with him. Kurt could still sense their frustration that their effort to get Hofmann to eliminate him had failed. What had once been admiration for his heroic feat of escaping England had withered and died as resentment and jealously grew in its place. Klaus and Jürgen rarely spoke to Kurt these days but their looks spoke of disdain and a desire to see him fall. Kurt reprimanded himself for not keeping his mouth shut. It was dangerous to trust anyone here. Everybody was out to save their own skin, Kurt included.

"I want to come too," said Dieter that evening when the other two weren't in the room.

"Good. We'll leave when those idiots who we have to share our room with get back and fall asleep."

Kurt's stomach gurgled with anxiety as he lay in the dark, listening out to determine if Klaus and Jürgen on the upper bunks had drifted off. It seemed forever since they had all gone to bed. Quietly he slid out of his bunk and tapped Dieter on the arm. Taking their clothes and shoes, they gingerly opened the door and slipped out into the unlit corridor where by feel and touch they dressed before going out into the courtyard.

Like a searchlight, a full moon illuminated it. A solitary lamp shone from the upper window of the tower but thankfully Hofmannn wasn't standing at the window. Kurt made a sign with his arm. Pulses racing, they advanced towards the exit gate. In the stillness of the night, the movement of the gravel beneath their feet sounded dangerously loud.

Kurt's shoulders were pinched together in dread of a shout to stop, of Hofmann suddenly appearing and blocking their way. Every muscle in Kurt's body was taut. They needed to get out of here unnoticed if they were to have any prospect of escaping. There was absolutely no way they would succeed if pursuit of them began the moment that they left. Once through the gates, Kurt relaxed a little.

"Where now?" asked Dieter.

"Down the road."

A rush of freedom invigorated Kurt from head to toe. He was out. Out of that hell hole which he had endured for the last three years. Having to live a lie, and always unable to reveal his true feelings, that place had come close to robbing him of humanity and empathy.

After a while, the two youths could see a beam of light sweeping back and forth in a semi-circle in the direction in which they were headed.

"Why are you taking us this way? We could be seen."

"We'll keep out of its range. It's coming from some kind of camp. When I arrived, they told me to get off the train just outside it. The train continued on in. Apart from the soldiers' carriage, it was pulling cattle wagons. Probably food for the army. I'm gambling that when the wagons leave, they will be empty and we can jump aboard for a ride across Germany. That way Hofmann's never going to be able to catch us."

"You're gambling?" Dieter's voice croaked like a frog. "If you're wrong, we'll be stuck only a few kilometres away. Hofmann will catch us easily. I can't believe I agreed to come." He sounded as if he might be about to burst into tears.

"We'll wait until dawn. If no train's come out by then, we'll start walking."

"This is terrible. Just awful."

Kurt saw red. With both hands, he grabbed Dieter by the collar.

"Shut up and stop whining will you! If you give up before we've hardly started of course it'll end in failure. You have got to be positive. Moaning will achieve nothing, and remember what the alternative was. The Russian front. Do you really think that you would have remained alive for more than a few minutes? If you think I'm wrong then go back before anyone wakes up and notices that you've left. I don't care."

Kurt released his grip and carried on down the road, breathing heavily with anger. He didn't bother to check if Dieter was following. Kurt too was anxious but Dieter's complaining only made him feel worse. It wasn't long until he heard Dieter panting close behind him.

Reaching the railway line, they crouched down by the side of it and waited. Eventually, in the east above the camp, the blanket of the night sky began to hole. Tension nudged its way in between the two of them, an unwelcome guest poking them with its sharp elbows to remind them that they would be easy to capture.

No train appeared. Soon it would be broad daylight and their disappearance would be noticed. It would take only minutes for a vehicle to get here from the monastery.

"We should start walking," said Dieter.

"No, let's wait a bit longer. The train driver's probably just waking now."

"If there's one even in there," muttered Dieter quietly so that Kurt didn't hear him.

The sun rose over the camp, its rays chasing away shadow and safety. It was the most powerful searchlight of all. Sweating despite the chill of early morning, Kurt knew that he'd left it too late for them to get far enough away to have a decent chance of success. The chains of panic wound themselves tightly around him.

"Okay, let's go. We'll need to run as fast as we can. If you can't keep up, I can't wait for you."

"Hang on," said Dieter. "What's that noise?"

It seemed to travel down the track towards them. A faint vibration which was becoming louder with each passing second. Soon they could see it. Their metal saviour blowing out thick smoke behind the barbed wire. The gates opened.

They threw themselves back down in the overgrown grass. As the locomotive began passing by, the clatter of it went right through them like a drill.

"Now," urged Kurt.

They jumped up and clambered onto a wagon that had its door slid back. Once on board, they pulled the door until it was almost closed, leaving only enough room to slide it back open again when they got off. It took a while for their eyes to adjust to the dim light inside. Although it stunk of urine and excrement, they didn't care. The train was gradually picking up speed. Spontaneously, they shook hands.

"See, I told you," said Kurt.

Then unexpectedly, he froze.

"What's the matter?"

Dieter turned. Someone was sitting in the corner, head down and arms clutched around their knees.

"Who are you?" asked Kurt.

A face looked up at them, the whites of the eyes wide with fear. It appeared to be that of a young woman about their age. Dressed in striped pyjamas, she had the shortest of hair as though it had all been cut off not long ago. She gave no reply. "It's all right. We're not going to hurt you." Still she said nothing. "I'm Kurt and this is Dieter."

"Karolina." The word dropped from her mouth quietly as if saying it was a crime.

"Where are you going? Are you escaping?"

Karolina said nothing.

"We are," said Dieter. "We want to go west. Reach the Americans."

"Shh!" hissed Kurt but Dieter's openness had reassured her.

"I wanted to get out of the camp."

"Is it a KLV?" Seeing the confusion on her face, Dieter added, "For evacuees from the bombings."

"No, they kill people there." She spoke in a disturbingly matter of fact manner as if she had observed so much which was barbaric that she no longer had the ability to display emotion.

"What for?"

"What for? When have they ever needed a reason?"

"Are you Jewish?" asked Dieter.

"No."

"Why were you in there then?"

"When Germany invaded Poland, they took me away from my parents. It happened to all the children in my town. They sorted us into groups to decide who was sufficiently Aryan and who was not. They must have thought me suitable. They told me I was lucky, that I would be "Germanized", that I must forget the past and had a bright future in front of me. As if that is the case when you've been torn away from those you love. I was sent to live with a family in Germany. They treated me like a slave and beat me. In the end, I couldn't stand it any longer so I ran away. I was caught and sent to the camp."

"But you said that they killed people in there."

"Yes. Most they kill only minutes after they arrive. Even though they have a pretend station with a schedule showing trains leaving to other places, and a fake restaurant to calm people's fears. They march them off to the gas chambers. I was strong and healthy compared to most of them so they put me to work." She noticed the two of them staring at the contradiction conveyed by her pitifully thin frame which made her clothes appear several sizes too big for her. "I was when I arrived. They don't give you enough to eat. I knew that I'd soon be too weak to work so they'd kill me as well. Sneaking out on the train was my only chance of survival."

"Don't they check the wagons before the train leaves?"

"Of course, always. I stood against the inside wall of the wagon by the sliding door. It wasn't much of a plan, but there was no other way. I was desperate to get out. Fortunately, the guard didn't do a very good job. He only looked in from the outside. He couldn't be bothered to step inside, or maybe he didn't want to because of the smell. They make some of us hose down the wagons after each load of new prisoners arrives, but the stench of them being forced to relieve themselves where they stand, packed in so tightly that no one can move, is ingrained in the wood."

Kurt and Dieter sat contemplating what Karolina had described. Even after seeing so many newsreels of battle, her account shocked them to their core. Kurt thought of his journey here from France. Of all those wagons which must have been full of families being transported to their death, treated as if animals on their way to the abattoir. It was beyond belief, beyond horrific.

They travelled on in silence for quite some time until any of them spoke again.

"Where will you go?" asked Kurt

"I don't know. I will have to live from minute to minute. Hope for the best. That's all I can do."

All day they remained on the train, putting a considerable distance between them and Hofmann. Yet they remained in danger. Conspicuous in their Hitler Youth uniforms, Kurt fully expected them to be challenged and ordered to explain what they were doing should someone find them. Each time the train stopped, Dieter and Kurt listened out for the approach of guards, ready to jump out and run. Kurt didn't think that Karolina would be able to do the same.

But there were no inspections. When terror came the next day, it wasn't from where they would have expected.

CHAPTER 15

A sound which Kurt recognised from when he had lived in London, tore through the air, hurting his eardrums and obliterating the reassuring rhythm of the train while it had chuntered along. Their wagon jerked and shuddered violently before leaving the tracks and careering over rough ground, tossing them about like leaves in an autumnal storm as they sought unsuccessfully for something that they could cling to. It came to a sudden halt and toppled over, catapulting them against its side. Winded but surprisingly uninjured save for a few cuts, and bruises which would appear later, Kurt looked at the other two bundled in a heap near him.

"Are you all right?"

"Yes," came two replies.

Kurt reached up to grab what, until moments ago, had been the side of the wagon but was now its top. Pulling himself up by his arms, he managed to push back the sliding door and surveyed the world outside. Other wagons lay strewn about like a child's train set kicked over in a fit of temper. The engine and the carriage which would have been transporting any guards was a twisted entanglement of metal and flames. Satisfied that no one could have survived, Kurt dropped back down.

"Luckily for us, it looks like the bomb hit the front of the train. We need to get away from here before anyone comes."

"I don't think I have the strength to haul myself up there," said Karolina.

"Don't worry. I'll climb up and Dieter can lift you up to me."

Kurt got himself positioned with one leg dangling inside the wagon and the other on the outside. Dieter placed his hands around Karolina's waist and raised her upwards as Kurt leaned down to reach her arms and pull her towards him. He helped her balance with a leg either side just as he had.

Dropping to the ground, Kurt told her to jump. Karolina did so, collapsing like a rag doll at his feet. Dieter followed. Moving away from what remained of the train, they melted into the forest as shouts in the distance closed in.

Squatting in the undergrowth, they watched soldiers come running along the track towards the wreckage. It seemed that they hadn't been spotted. Silently as wolves, the three of them stole away.

Finding a stream, the young fugitives satiated their deep thirst. However, hunger was a torment which they couldn't banish. It had become their annoying travelling companion, always there demanding attention. As night approached, they set off again. Kurt led the way, then Dieter, with Karolina following in the rear.

"The last station name that I saw was Mainz," said Kurt. "I don't know how far the Allies have got, but the French border must be less than a hundred kilometres away. Three nights walking should get us there."

"What if they haven't got that far?" asked Dieter.

"In that case, we head towards the coast until we reach them."

There was a soft noise behind them as if a squirrel had fallen from out of a tree and landed on the leaves underfoot. They turned to see Karolina kneeling there in the golden glow cast by the sinking sun through the gaps between the trees.

"You should go on without me. I can't walk any further."

Her eyes were sunken into her skull and her skin a deathly white, features which they hadn't truly appreciated in the semi-darkness of the railway wagon or the commotion of earlier.

"No, you'll die or be captured if we abandon you here. Climb on my back. Dieter and I can take turns carrying you."

Kurt crouched down for Karolina so that she could put her arms around his neck. Not much heavier than a sack of potatoes, he could feel her bones digging into him through her threadbare clothing as he walked. Yet her weary head on his shoulder brought back to him the power of a human touch. It reminded him that it had been too long since he had felt the security of his mother's hug.

Come dawn, they were in a land of undulating hills with good forest cover. It was the Germany of fairytale books as if the war was a million miles away. Beyond the forest, neat rows of vines cascaded down slopes towards the occasional house.

"With any luck the grape harvest won't have started," said Dieter.

They left Karolina sitting on the forest floor and began going down a row, careful to keep their heads beneath the top of the vines to avoid detection. Picking grapes, they stuffed them into their mouths as quickly as they possibly could, not even bothering to spit out the pips or wipe off the juice soon running down their chins. The sweetness was sublime and renewing. It was the nectar of the gods. After they'd had their fill, they returned to Karolina, transporting grapes in their shirts pulled out from their shorts to make a suitable carrier. Ravenous, she gobbled them up just as quickly as they had.

"Oh, that's the most wonderful thing that I've eaten in ages. It's like dying and waking up in heaven. Thank you."

Not being quite so hungry relaxed them. They had the energy to talk.

"You never told me why you are running away,"

said Karolina.

"We were at a Hitler Youth camp. They wanted to send us to fight the Russians. We're fifteen but even boys who are only eleven and twelve, they're sending them too." said Dieter. "How old are you?"

"Seventeen."

Dieter looked surprised. Karolina appeared to be pre-pubescent. Her half-starved body had left her without curves of any kind. However, the pain reflected in her eyes spoke of someone much older than a teenager, someone who had witnessed unspeakable acts of cruelty.

"What do you plan to do when you reach the front line?"

"I hope I can go somewhere safe, and when this terrible war is over, I'll start searching for my family. My sister was sent to Germany like me but I don't know where. They separated us when we got off the train. And my brother was put with a group of boys before we left Warsaw. I have no idea where they were taken. Each day I pray that they're all still alive. My mother and father too. I tell God that I'll never ask him for anything ever again if only he will let me see them."

Kurt realised that he was fortunate by comparison. If he survived, he would know where to go to find his mother. Karolina's task sounded nigh on impossible, her family broken into so many pieces and scattered like the wind. If they had lived, it would be a miracle. Locating them would require another one.

Having eaten, they all experienced an interval of relative contentment. Soon, however, they were suffering stomach cramps from over indulging on grapes, and spent a great deal of the day disappearing to separate parts of the forest.

Come night, they set off once again and moved out into the open. Kurt and Dieter discarded their shoes. Blisters on their feet had been rubbed red raw. The stab of stones and pine needles was jarring but less constant. A harvest moon hung before them like a beacon of hope, caressing the land in a gentleness which its inhabitants had long forgotten. On the horizon, the sky lit up with intermittent flashes of light and the sound of anti-aircraft fire. The noise of exploding bombs reverberated through the air like thunder. Kurt wondered if they were close to their goal or if it was instead a bombing raid launched from afar.

They could see the silhouette of a town ahead. Kurt decided to approach it to look for a road sign to confirm if they were moving in the correct direction. In so far as he could, he kept to the darkest corners, creeping along like an enemy soldier seeking to avoid attracting sniper fire. He didn't find any signs so he proceeded farther in, thinking that a shopfront might give a clue as to their location.

In a small square a fountain bubbled, temporarily calming his nerves until he looked beyond it and saw three bodies hanging from gibbets.

Unable to overcome his curiosity, Kurt moved closer. The spectacle he witnessed stirred his gut. Three teenagers, just like him, swung almost imperceptibly in the light breeze. Three in their Hitler Youth outfits. Three who would have wanted to live, not die before their sixteenth birthday. The age Kurt would reach sometime soon, or maybe he already had. There was no calendar which he could check.

Shaken, Kurt retreated to an alleyway. If he had ever doubted it at all, he knew now that this would be his fate if he failed. There would be no second chances. Success or death were the only two possible outcomes.

Looking up, he saw the name of the shop that he was standing outside of included the name of this macabre town where adolescents were strung up and left there to intimidate the population. Noting that they were still moving west, he scurried out of town and back to the safety of the woods. Kurt didn't mention what he had seen to the others, adding to their stress wouldn't help.

The day after as dawn arrived, they crossed into France but a part of France still occupied by the Nazis, apparent from the flags draped from buildings like crosses on doors in medieval times warning of the plague.

Another night of walking brought them near to the city of Metz. They began to skirt around it until they reached a barrier which Kurt hadn't factored into his calculations. Fast flowing and dark as oil, a river blocked their way. They walked alongside it in a futile search for a way across. There was a bridge but they could see little orange lights emanating from the tips of the cigarettes belonging to soldiers guarding the crossing. They retreated not knowing what to do. It seemed a certainty that all bridges would be manned.

"Maybe we can find a rowing boat," suggested Kurt. They looked without success until Dieter called out.

"Come look. There's a tree trunk lying in the water here, jammed against the bank. It's big enough for us all to sit astride and float across. Kurt, let's both find a tree branch before we go so that we have something to paddle with."

The log rolled alarmingly while they clambered on to it. Kurt battled his fear of drowning as they pushed their legs against the river bank and drifted into the flow, picking up surprising

speed as the water caught them. The branches proved to be utterly ineffective as paddles. The river had its own powerful momentum, carrying them like flotsam down the middle. It seemed that they would be taken for miles if they weren't thrown off first. Soon the log had turned one hundred and eighty degrees and they were travelling facing backwards.

Craning their necks, they could see a bridge up ahead. It was the same one which they had backed away from earlier. There was nothing they could do as they hurtled towards it. They would have to hope that none of the soldiers were watching the river below them. As the trunk neared the arches of the bridge, the current divided. Hitting the wall of an arch head on at speed, they were nearly thrown off. However, it had the advantage of slowing them down and changing their direction of travel.

Not far beyond the bridge, the trunk tired of playing with them and came to rest against the bank. They had crossed successfully, albeit too close to the bridge for comfort. Hearts pumping, they crawled up the river bank as quietly as they possibly could, fearfully looking to their left for any sign that they had been noticed. Fate smiled upon them and let them go. They slipped off into the night and continued edging around the city, gratefully flopping to the ground once back among tree cover.

Hunger stalked them still. Ever present, they were unable to shake it off. Food was rarely absent from their thoughts. Deprived of calories, it was becoming ever more of an effort to put one foot in front of the other. Even Karolina now felt heavy to carry. Lying down and not getting back up again became an appealing prospect. The three of them rarely exchanged a word. It had become too much of an effort to do so. The diminishing strength which they had left, they reserved for walking.

As day broke, Dieter who had briefly disappeared

came hobbling back, his face no longer pained and instead a picture of unexpected jubilation.

"There's an orchard beyond the field over there. There could be apples or pears for us to eat."

"We should wait until nightfall," cautioned Kurt.

"You can if you like. The countryside's deserted, no one will see us. Karolina?"

She nodded and climbed onto his back. Kurt watched the two of them go, Dieter occasionally stumbling as if he might fall over from the exertion. It wasn't long until the thought of sustenance proved an irresistible temptation to Kurt also.

The orchard was behind a high stone wall. Dieter pushed on the wooden door built into the wall. Once the door must have been maroon, now only a little colouring remained on the rotting wood. Inside was their garden of Eden. Pear trees, maybe twenty or more. Grass had grown tall around them. It was a place forgotten.

"Stop!" shouted Kurt. "There's a house beyond here. We could be seen."

"It doesn't look like anyone is living there," said Dieter. "The shutters are all closed."

Karolina had already picked a pear from a low hanging branch. The others did the same. The fruit wasn't ripe. Not succulent, it was hard on their jaws yet none of them were in the least deterred. It was food to fill that empty ache which they had carried like stones in their stomachs for days.

Kurt was well into his third pear when it

114

happened.

CHAPTER 16

Like a tiny asteroid, a shell hit the house beyond the orchard, decimating a considerable amount of masonry. Looking back through the open gate to the orchard, they could see tanks lumbering resolutely in their direction.

More explosives flew above, this time from the opposite direction. The smoke created on impact obscured the advancing armour. Unwittingly, they had placed themselves in the middle of a battlefield between the two opposing forces.

"I think we've found the front line," said Karolina without a hint of irony.

"We can't stay here. We'll have to take our chances and go forward. Dieter, if you carry Karolina, I'll go in front and navigate a route through the fighting."

"What if they shoot us?"

"We're going to have to take that risk. If we remain where we are, we'll have tanks on top of us in no time. And if we survive, they'll hang us. Those are German tanks. In that town I went into the other night, three boys our age were dangling from a rope."

Dieter didn't require any more persuasion. Using her arms, Karolina shuffled backwards on her bottom as Dieter went to pick her up.

"No, you must go without me. You need to run. I'll slow you down."

"We've come this far together, we can't leave you now," said Kurt.

"You won't have to, you can get the Americans to come and rescue me. I'll stay hidden here in the long grass." Kurt and Dieter exchanged glances, uncertain what they should do. "Go. You're wasting valuable time."

They chose not to argue with her and exited the orchard from a door in the wall near the house. They went around the side of it. Tanks were coming at them. As they ran forwards, the ground transformed itself into something akin to an underground volcano. Dislodged by explosions, mud and stones were thrust upwards and outwards with great force, raining down upon them as if the earth itself had joined the fight. More than once they were knocked off their feet. Each time, they got back up instantly. Out here, they would either be crushed by tank treads or blown to pieces.

By luck rather than judgment, they got past the tanks without either event happening. On the brow of a small rise, they could see soldiers a short distance away.

"We're surrendering," shouted Kurt as they got closer, hands high in the air.

"Be careful," shouted one of the soldiers to his comrades. "I've heard that some of these Hitler Youth bastards wait for you to get near and then detonate a grenade. They're happy to die just so long as they take as many of us with them as possible."

"Don't move a muscle or we'll shoot," ordered another.

Kurt was relieved that the men were speaking English. They had American accents. He translated for Dieter.

"Hey! Keep your mouth shut."

"I was just repeating your order. He doesn't speak English."

"Well, don't. Brooks, search them."

The man used the end of his rifle to do so, prodding aggressively to determine if they had concealed anything on their person. A circle of other soldiers stood around them a short way back, weapons at the ready.

"They're clean."

"Okay, take them to the compound."

"Sir," said Kurt. "There's a girl with us, hiding in the orchard behind the big house."

"The house ain't there no more."

Kurt twisted his neck. All that remained was a mound of rubble. The orchard walls too had collapsed. The pear trees were blackened, their leaves and fruit gone, supplanted by the burned out shell of a German tank. Vomit rose in the back of Kurt's throat. If only they had brought her too, she would have been safe by now. Karolina had come so close to freedom. After all that she had endured, it was so desperately sad that it should have ended like this, at the last hurdle. Kurt hoped against hope that she might still be alive, but it seemed most unlikely that anyone could have survived such an inferno.

Hands on their heads, the boys were marched off in single file. As they passed through a small town, women and old men watched them pass by. Some shouted. Kurt didn't understand what they were saying, but their virulent tone made it obvious that whatever their message it wasn't words of welcome. After four years of brutal occupation that was hardly surprising.

On the far side of the town they arrived at their destination, a fenced enclosure which smelled as though until recently it must have been used to keep pigs. There were already German soldiers in there, seated on the ground while a guard watched over them.

"Look," said one of the Germans to his colleagues. "They've started using the Kindergarten to fight our battles."

That produced some belly laughs. Dieter and Kurt went to sit in the opposite corner from where the others were congregated, not wanting to be the centre of attention any longer. They weren't, the men had already lost interest in them.

A heavy rain shower fell from a leaden sky, soaking

them right through. Kurt didn't mind. He had succeeded. He had survived. Soon he would be on his way back to England and freedom. For the first time in three years he'd be truly free, free from the rabid rantings of Hofmann and his gang, and free to enjoy what was left of his adolescence. Kurt fondly imagined his mother being there to greet him on his release, newspaper reporters jockeying to talk to him, his story a national sensation, and this time a true one.

"It's all right for you," muttered Dieter, observing his friend's far away grin. "You'll be a hero once again. I'll be stuck in a prison camp with this lot for who knows how long."

"I'll put in a good word for you. Tell them how you were abused, forced to do things against your will. I'm sure you'll be well treated. England's not like Germany."

"I hope so. Anyway, I shouldn't be grumbling. At least I'm alive. Poor Karolina. We shouldn't have left her. It was wrong of us."

"I know." The smile had gone from Kurt's face. "I feel exactly the same way."

They sat in silence for several minutes, guilt weighing down upon them. They could never undo what they had done. A moment of selfishness. What had been the point of carrying her for days to leave her like they had. They would have to live with their remorse and their sense of shame for a long time. Maybe forever.

A line of recently captured men arrived, interrupting their introspection. The man leading them surveyed those already there in a contemptuous fashion. He had an aquiline nose and beady eyes which suited his haughty manner.

"Decided to give up too?" asked one of the men already there.

"Absolutely not," retorted the officer "We were surrounded."

"Sounds like surrender to me."

"How dare you address an officer of the Wehrmacht in that manner. Name?"

"Name? What are you going to do? Report me for insubordination? We're losing. We're prisoners now, rank is irrelevant. This war will soon be over, and you and your kind will be consigned to the dung heap of history."

The officer had become a pressure cooker about to blow off its lid.

"You will pay for your impudence! You are a disgrace to the Reich. Not like those two lads over there." Kurt and Dieter compressed their necks into their shoulders. They didn't want to be noticed and questioned about how they had come to be here. "It is our young people that will lead us to victory, not defeatist traitors like you. I'm Major Engel, and I never forget a face."

"His name's Kessel," volunteered another prisoner. A GI entered the compound.

"Everybody up. We're moving out."

"When are you going to tell the Americans?" asked Dieter as they walked along, two by two.

"Just as soon as I get a proper chance."

After a few miles, the POWs arrived at a station and were herded onto freight wagons. All through the night they travelled. Halting next morning, there was a freshness coming through the gaps in the wooden planks. Outside, squawking pierced the air.

"Seagulls," said Kurt. "We must have reached the coast."

Blinking at the brightness as the metal doors were slid open, Kurt's spirits soared. The nightmare of recent years would soon be at an end. A short distance away, an enormous hulk of grey metal waited on the quayside. Under armed guard, they were escorted to it. Once aboard, they were left free to wander the deck. Looking out to sea, Kurt couldn't see the English coast, but he knew it could only be a matter of fifty miles at most, and probably less. He wanted to shout out with joy, tell everyone that Kurt Ziegler was going home.

"I'm going to have a word with that soldier over there," he told Dieter once the boat was out at sea.

He approached the man who appeared to be in charge, a man who could well have been only a few years older than him.

"Excuse me, sir."

"Yeah." His tone was one of complete disinterest.

"I know I may look German in this uniform but

I'm not. I'm English. I was kidnapped and taken to Germany, told I must fight or be killed. I escaped and walked to the front line so that I could surrender and get back home."

"Is that right?" The man chewed on his gum while he looked Kurt up and down.

"Yes, when we get to England, you can let me go. You can contact my mother in London if you need to. She'll be able to confirm who I am."

"We ain't going to England. We're taking you lucky sons of bitches to the United States of America. England's already overflowing with Nazi POWs so we're helping them out."

"But-"

"Stop bothering me, kid. I grant you speak good English but I don't wanna hear any more sob stories. Now get before I have you locked up for the rest of the voyage."

CHAPTER 17

"Are you feeling seasick?" asked Dieter.

Kurt did indeed feel nauseous. Never for one moment had he thought that his account wouldn't be accepted.

"He didn't believe me."

"Well, you can just tell someone else when we land in England."

"No, I can't. They're taking us to America."

"America?" Dieter was as surprised as Kurt. "I've always wanted to go there, see what it's like. It'll be an adventure," he added in an effort to cheer his friend up. "And once the war's ended, you'll get to go home then. It's not like you're going to come to any harm, is it?"

"No, I suppose not."

"Wow, America," repeated Dieter.

At first, Kurt couldn't believe that having been so close to getting home, he was now going to be farther away from it than he had ever been. By the time their crossing was nearing its end, Kurt had reconciled himself to his fate. America had to be a big improvement on the last few years. Like Dieter, he too was fascinated by the USA from the movies of 'Cowboys and Indians' which he'd seen as a boy. He didn't expect a POW camp was likely to be a bed of roses, but if the food on the ship was anything to go by, Americans ate a whole lot better than he had at both the KLV in occupied Poland and back in England. And Dieter was right, he was safe now.

Everyone was ordered on deck to watch their arrival. The Germans stood in silent awe as the vessel sailed past the skyscrapers of Manhattan and close to the Statue of Liberty before turning and docking at the port of Hoboken on the mainland opposite the western side of Manhattan. This didn't look like the poor and backward country incapable of beating Germany that they had been lectured about, a land of degenerates and racial impurity destined to implode at any moment.

Disembarking, they were led into a cavernous empty warehouse and told to sit on the floor. An icy wind blew off the water through the open space where the doors had been slid back. Something wet landed on Kurt's head. Looking up at the metal rafters, he saw that they were lined with pigeons. Removing the deposit with his hand as best he could, he rubbed his palm on the concrete floor. He wasn't enjoying his first experience on American soil.

"If they ask for our names, I think we should change them as a precaution. What do you think?" said Dieter.

"Yes, let's," agreed Kurt.

Commanded to get up and form a line, they were led to a room where two men called them forward one by one, spraying each prisoner with delousing powder. Then they were questioned about their identity. Dieter had made up a Hamburg address for Kurt to give. Directed to leave through a door at the back of the building, they were told to board a waiting train. All were astonished to see that they were to be travelling not in freight wagons as they had anticipated but Pullman cars.

Dieter and Kurt secured themselves seats facing each other. This was more like setting off on a luxury holiday than being detained. They grinned, unable to believe their good fortune. Two men came and sat across the aisle from them and immediately the atmosphere darkened. One they recognised instantly, Major Engel from the initial holding camp in France.

Shortly after departure, they were to be surprised again when they were offered sandwiches and beverages served by a black man.

"As the Führer has told us, Negroes and Jews are like a disease in this country. If we don't win the war, a nation of half breeds will be no match for the Soviets," said Engel to his colleague.

Kurt and Dieter must surely have regretted that they had been staring at the man as he spoke.

"Ah, the two boys from France, just outside Metz."

"Yes, sir," said Dieter.

"Names?"

"Braun, sir."

"Brandt, sir."

"Tell me, what unit were you with?"

"Unit." Dieter repeated the word. Kurt recognised it as a cry for help.

"We don't know, sir," he intervened. "We ran away from home to the front to be of service. The officer we met gave us guns and told us to follow others. Unfortunately, we got separated from them and captured."

"Well, at least you tried to do your duty. Some on this train preferred to be taken prisoner rather than do theirs."

"Sir." An American guard had arrived. "We have more comfortable accommodation for officers at the front of the train."

Engel looked at the man blankly. Without thinking, Kurt translated for him.

"You speak English?" asked Engel.

"I studied it at school."

"That's useful to know. I may need your assistance at the camp they are sending us to. Heil Hitler."

Automatically, Kurt and Dieter jumped to their feet and reciprocated the arm gesture as Engel and his companion moved.

"Damn. I should have kept my big mouth shut," said Kurt.

Their journey continued all night and the following day.

"This country is never ending," exclaimed Dieter. "How did Hitler ever think that he could beat them."

Gradually, lush greenery surrendered to a more open, arid, and dusty landscape where clouds like huge ships sailed past above them as if explorers on an unknown ocean searching for a port in an endless sky. Arriving at Huntsville in Texas, they were walked four abreast the few miles to the camp. Rivulets of sweat tickled Kurt's torso as they trickled down his body. While in New York the whisper of approaching winter had carried a sharp chill, here the climate fried them. He enjoyed the novelty of feeling hotter than he ever had in his life. In time, he would come to dislike its energy-sapping relentlessness.

Although behind high chain-link fencing topped with barbed wire, the camp wasn't oppressive in the way which the monastery had been. Inside the long huts were bunkbeds considerably more comfortable than those at the KLV, and there was more than ample space between them. Officers had their own separate quarters. Several of the ordinary soldiers who Kurt and Dieter shared their accommodation with were quite open about the fact that they didn't support Nazism. That many must have voted for Hitler or otherwise been complicit in the rise of National Socialism was quickly forgotten and blamed on others. However, there remained some who still seemed committed to the cause.

"We should keep our opinions to ourselves. I don't trust that Engel. He's probably already got his spies in here," cautioned Dieter.

Engel and other senior German officers insisted on maintaining military discipline, requiring the POWs to march to and from meals, and when required to assemble for daily roll calls. At the end of roll call one morning, Kurt heard the man call his name.

"Brandt." Engel's presence was like an ice cube dropped down the back of his shirt.

"Yes, sir," said Kurt standing to attention, a reflex after his years at the KLV.

"I want you to accompany me to the camp commandant's office so that you can translate."

Once again, Kurt cursed himself for having been so stupid to reveal his language skills. He wanted nothing more than to be ignored by that man. Now he would be at his beck and call whenever he needed someone to speak English for him, unable to refuse and at risk of his past being discovered.

Engel had a litany of complaints concerning the treatment of the officers. The camp commandant was polite but firm in dismissing them all. Unaccustomed to not getting what he wanted, Engel left the meeting in a foul temper. Kurt followed, unsure if he was dismissed.

"Why are you still here, boy?" snapped Engel.

"Sorry, sir. I didn't know if you required me for anything else."

"No. Be gone."

Other than officers, who couldn't be required to work under the terms of the Geneva Convention, everyone else was taken off camp six days a week to work on local farms. With most young men in the locality off fighting in the Pacific or Europe, there was a labour shortage. Early each morning, the prisoners climbed onto trucks which toured the area, dropping them at various points. Nearly all welcomed being kept busy and the change of scene. Kurt and Dieter were assigned to work on a cotton plantation together with a few others.

Although it was November, it remained hot. Working topless, they soon acquired a tan. Kurt had never looked so healthy. As an English speaker, he got to act as go-between, explaining what needed to be done as relayed by Al Fitzpatrick, the owner. The man had a face of cracked leather, weatherbeaten like his land. He squinted even when not in direct sunlight. No doubt he'd had to spend so much of his life doing so that it had become his natural state.

"You sure speak good English for a German."

"My mother's English."

"That would explain it then."

Kurt had decided not to reveal his true story to anyone in view of the poor reception the last time that he had done so. He now appreciated how it could all sound unbelievable to someone else, a young man's imagination run wild. And he feared if the other POWs got word of what he was saying that the news would get back to Engel. The war surely couldn't last that much longer, and when they were freed he would raise the matter again.

Several black men worked on the same plantation. They gave the POWs stares of curiosity. White people out working like they did wasn't something which they were used to seeing.

As Kurt stood mopping his brow in the midday sun, one of them in a wide-brimmed straw hat came up to him. He moved awkwardly as if his joints hurt, which they probably did after a lifetime of manual labour.

"Did you need some water? The sun can be awful fierce. If you don't drink enough, it'll make you sick."

"Yes please."

"You wait here while I go get you some."

"But you've got a bucket of water right there."

"We've been taking water out of it."

"So?"

"White folk refuse to drink from the same place that we do."

"Why?"

"You'd have to ask them."

"Well, I think that's stupid."

"Never thought I'd hear a white person say that. You sure? We only have one cup."

"Of course, I'm sure. I thought America was the land of the free."

"It is. For white folk."

He shuffled a few steps, returning with a metal cup of water taken from the nearby bucket. Kurt guzzled the drink down.

"Where are all your young men?"

"Fighting the war. I got two boys somewhere in the Pacific. I pray they'll make it back, although they're gonna find it tough when they come home. They may have fought for their country but they'll still have to stay out of the whites only places, and make sure they never upset a white person if they don't want to end up swinging from a tree."

Kurt didn't know how to respond to that so he didn't. This wasn't the America he'd heard of.

The ringing of a bell signalled that there was food. The prisoners happily downed their tools. The black men continued working. They didn't get fed.

A young woman was handing out sandwiches. A dainty creature with a face that radiated warmth, her smile touched Kurt in a way that he didn't understand. When she looked at him with her dark eyes which were brilliant like onyx, a feeling of longing the likes of which he had never before experienced coursed through his veins.

CHAPTER 18

"Hi, I'm Jessie." The way she spoke was as mesmerising as her appearance. Her voice was big for someone so petite, unexpectedly husky yet undeniably sensual. Entranced, Kurt could do nothing but stare. "And you are?"

"I'm Kurt."

"You must be the one dad was telling me about. The English speaker."

"Yes."

"We're grateful to have you boys. We've been struggling with our men off fighting, though I guess you can't be too happy to be here."

"No, it's er…it's fine."

Conscious of other men behind him becoming impatient, Kurt moved on. While he sat eating, he stole furtive glances. Although in work clothes coated with dust, she looked like a goddess to him. Hair of jet black, which was piled on her head in the fashion of the day, had been styled to also cascade onto her shoulders. She was a revelation after years of an abysmal existence, the embodiment of a hope that life wouldn't always be one of fear and the complete lack of joy.

The bell sounded again. It was back to work. But as he dug the hard ground, there was an enthusiasm in Kurt's actions not present before.

Back at camp that evening, the POWs sat under the stars watching a Hollywood movie. It was a magical experience. Kurt went to bed that night happier than at any time since those distant days in Dulverton when he and Barb had sledged in the winter and fished in the summer. A time when, in retrospect, life had been so simple.

Keen to return to work the next day, Kurt went to the back of the line at lunch thinking he'd get more time to talk to Jessie. To his delight, she remembered him.

"Oh hi, I was wondering where you'd gotten to. Dad tells me your mom is English. Must be kind of tough for her living in Germany and all."

"Yeah." Kurt offered no detail.

"Are you going to the dance this Saturday?"

"Dance?"

"They're letting you guys out for the evening."

"I can't dance."

"That doesn't matter, there'll be a guy calling out what to do. It's country music, not a ball or anything fancy. You should come, I think you'd enjoy it."

The dance was held in a field outside town. Two men were playing a fiddle, another a banjo. Kurt's heart missed a beat when he saw Jessie. He'd never seen her in a dress, only the dungarees she wore for work. In her mascara and red lipstick, and a blue and white checked dress she was a vision of perfection.

"You came." Jessie looked genuinely happy to see him. "Come on, let's dance."

Kurt marvelled at America. Where else would they treat POWs like this? Certainly not in Germany, and he didn't imagine being a POW in England would be particularly pleasant.

They laughed as they danced, their eyes aglow. After several dances, Jessie suggested that they walk down to the creek. When she sat down beside it, he did too.

"Look up there, Kurt. Ain't it incredible?"

In the Texan night sky the Milky Way was clearly visible, a celestial promise of hope in the darkness that the bad times Kurt had endured were ending. A chorus of crickets sang in the warm air and toads played bass. All seemed right with the world in a way things never had since he was but a small child unaware of who he was, someone different from others.

"What will you do when the war's over? Go back to Germany?"

"I hadn't really thought about it. Do you have any plans?" said Kurt, quickly deflecting the question.

"Not really. Stay here, I guess. It's been kinda fun helping dad while Ron's away fighting."

"Ron?" Kurt's spirits plummeted. She already had a boyfriend.

"My brother, the apple of daddy's eye. When he gets back, I'll be stuck with all the cooking and cleaning again. Dad will want to fire our help to save money."

"What about your mother?"

"She got sick when we were little. They had to put her in an asylum. I haven't seen her for a while. She doesn't know who any of us are. It makes me sad if I visit her."

"That must be difficult for you."

For what to Kurt seemed too long an interval, they sat upright in silence. Only a few tantalising inches separated them. Kurt considered if he should cross that small space, which his mind was making appear so wide, and kiss her but he succumbed to his nerves They told him to remember what had happened when he had taken hold of Barb's hand. If he made a move he might ruin a perfect evening, they insisted. If only he were patient he could perhaps have a future that until now he had thought would never let him catch up with it.

Unexpectedly, he felt her. The gentle touch of her hand on his rough, calloused one, a soothing balm for a confused and battered soul. He turned his neck. Jessie's big eyes locked onto his and she leaned towards him. Her mouth was oh so soft and inviting, a tenderness that he had never experienced. The trauma of his past was temporarily buried in her kiss.

"Where'd you disappear to," asked Dieter as they walked back to camp.

"Nowhere."

"Well, it must have been somewhere. You missed a good time. American girls are so friendly, and they smell so good."

Kurt didn't respond. Jessie was his secret, a secret too precious to share even with Dieter. Although Kurt couldn't fathom what she could possibly see in him, still more boy than man and a prisoner with no prospects, he was deliriously happy that she appeared to like him.

Reaching their hut, they filed in with the others. The men were in boisterous good humour. Life was worth living once more. Their war was over and being imprisoned really wasn't that bad. One flicked the switch on the wall. Mosquitoes bobbed around under the bright, clinical light of the naked bulb.

When they saw him, there was a collective intake of breath. A man hung from one of the crossbeams in the ceiling. A chair lay on its side, kicked away to end his life.

"Why would he kill himself?" Dieter asked Kurt.

"Manfred Kessel wouldn't have committed suicide," answered a man next to them. "It's got to be Engel and those other crazy Nazi officers. I've heard that they've set up a kangaroo court to judge those considered traitors to the Reich. There was another so-called suicide in one of the other huts last week."

Kessel. Kurt remembered the name. The man near Metz in France who had earned Engel's enmity for disrespecting him. What the man next to him had said made perfect sense. Kessel wasn't the kind of person likely to kill himself. Kurt didn't know him but he'd seen him laughing and playing cards with his friends, and heard him enthusing about the future now this 'damn war' was in its final throes, and heard him say how he was looking forward to getting home to his wife and child.

Guards were called. They cut the rope and carried away the body. The light-hearted atmosphere of the evening went out with it. They hadn't left evil behind in Europe. Like a rat, it had jumped aboard ship with them.

Winter came, not that a Texan winter was what Kurt considered winter to be. There was no snow, and most of the time it was as warm as an English summer. They would be fed turkey twice in a month. The first time was to celebrate Thanksgiving and the next would be Christmas. For Kurt, it was a first. In England, even before the war turkey had been too expensive for most. His family used to dine on goose instead.

For the eighty cents a day the prisoners earned from working, they received payment by way of scrip rather than cash, which the authorities feared would have proved useful to those who might be planning to escape. Kurt used his earnings to buy candy, as Americans called sweets, and a fizzy brown drink that he had never had before coming to America but became a fan of with the first mouthful. Coca-Cola.

Kurt also traded some of his scrips for a wooden Christmas tree angel which one of the prisoners had carved and painted. It reminded Kurt of childhood Christmases at home in London which seemed like another lifetime now. On Christmas Eve, he gave the angel to Jessie. She was delighted with it, telling him that it would take pride of place on the family's Christmas tree.

Kurt hoped there might soon be another dance so that he could spend time alone again with her. Their regular meetings as she handed out lunch were short and unsatisfactory. In bed at night, Kurt fantasised about staying in America, and possibly marrying her one day.

He certainly didn't want to be returned to Germany, and England had become little more than a land of memories, the good ones outnumbered by the bad.

On New Year's Eve, a guard came to the hut to tell Kurt that he had a visitor. Following the man to the camp entrance, he was surprised to see Jessie at the gate.

"I've brought you some cookies I baked. I thought you and your friends could share them."

"Thank you." Kurt's tone and expression was downcast.

"What's wrong. Aren't you happy I came?"

"Yes, of course I am. It's just very frustrating being in here. I wish we could go into town and be like normal people."

"Me too. Things will soon be different. They say the war will be over in a few months and then we can." She kissed him quickly on the cheek in an embarrassed, self-conscious sort of way. "I gotta go now. Happy New Year."

Jessie was right. Things would soon be different. Different in a way which Kurt could never have imagined.

CHAPTER 19

A few days into 1945, new POWs arrived. Those already there watched them as they were marched in, curious to see these new arrivals. An officer led the column, his head proudly upright and his expression defiant. Dieter and Kurt kept their mouths shut but looked at each other in the same way as if a ghost had walked right through them. When the others dispersed, they stayed rooted to the spot, stunned.

"Hof-" Dieter choked on the word. Kurt nodded gravely. "I don't understand it. How could he be here? He was sending us to fight the Russians."

"Knowing Hofmann, he probably left everyone else to be massacred and fled west to save his own skin."

"Well, at least that means he'll want to keep quiet about you and me if he recognises us."

"Maybe, maybe not. One thing's for sure, we need to keep a low profile and stay out of his way."

Kurt slept fitfully that night. No longer did being here feel safe. He didn't share Dieter's view that Hofmann would ignore them for fear of being challenged of how he had come to be in the west and captured by the Americans. However, he reminded himself, the officers kept themselves to themselves most of the time. With luck, Hofmann wouldn't become aware of their presence. If the war ended soon, it would be all right, or would it? A sharp knife of fear ran down the length of his spine.

Kurt and Dieter learned to take precautions. They approached corners cautiously, ready to beat a hasty retreat if they should see their nemesis coming in their direction. Assembling for roll call each day, they stood at the back and kept their heads down. The lads avoided doing things where he was more likely to notice them. After a day's work, they stayed in their hut, even forgoing the movie nights which they so enjoyed. They were as enamoured with the Hollywood stars as the rest of the prisoners but it was too dangerous to go. The officers nearly always attended, soaking up American culture which they supposedly held in contempt.

A summons to meet with Engel several weeks later had Kurt on edge. His legs had become lead weights when he arrived at the officers' hut. Hofmann might well be in there. It was where he lived. Kurt hung around outside, seeking to postpone the inevitable. The door was flung open. "What took you so long? Did you not get my order?" barked Engel.

"I'm sorry, sir. I had a call of nature to attend to."

"Hmm," grunted Engel. "Come, I have a meeting with the commandant. Next week is the Führer's birthday. I want the men to be allowed to celebrate and display their loyalty. It is only right. After all, the Americans make so much fuss about George Washington, a man of insignificance compared to our leader."

The request was refused.

"Impudent man," raged Engel outside the office. Kurt made to go. "Wait! I have a message that I want delivered to Hut 3. You can come back with me and collect it."

Kurt halted as they reached the officers' hut.

"Shall I wait here, sir?"

"No, come inside."

With dread Kurt entered, hunched as if he was about to be ambushed. The hut interior was different to the others. There were armchairs and a desk at which Engel sat down and began writing his note. A door led from the room to separate sleeping quarters. A couple of officers were seated in armchairs. One was buried behind a newspaper, the other smoking and looking bored was thankfully not Hofmann.

There was the rattle of paper as a page was turned. The reader lowered the newspaper slightly, revealing the man's eyes. Instantly, Kurt knew who it was. Kurt quickly dropped his head to hide his face. Engel came over from the desk and stood in the space between Kurt and Hofmann.

"There. Take it."

"Thank you, sir. Heil Hitler."

Kurt exited as fast as he could, exhaling with relief as soon as he got outside. It seemed likely that Hofmann hadn't recognised him. A mere errand boy, not worthy of his attention. But it had without doubt been a close call.

Soon there was news to lighten Kurt's mood.

"Hey, I spoke to one of the guys in charge at the camp yesterday," Jessie told him as he got his lunch at the end of the line as usual. "He says I can take you into town tomorrow evening if you'd like. Just you and me."

"Really?"

"Yes, really. So?"

"That would be lovely."

"I'll see you at the gate then. At six."

Back at camp that evening there was a lesson about democracy. The American government hoped by teaching the men how their system of government worked that when the prisoners went back to Germany, they could be at the forefront of helping establish a functioning democracy. Once the war ended, there would be Soviet agents trying their upmost to engineer a communist dictatorship, of that the US authorities were convinced. After twelve years as a one party state and the political turmoil of the 1920s, most ordinary Germans had little concept of or faith in democratic government.

Coming around the corner of a building after the lecture, Kurt jumped, startled by the sight of someone else.

"Is something wrong, Brandt? You appear nervous."

"No, sir. You surprised me."

"Attending the talk on so-called democracy were you? It's a pernicious system, manipulated by Jews and Bolsheviks. It ruined Germany," said Engel.

"Yes, sir."

"You know, Brandt, I've never really thanked you for your assistance, translating my words to that buffoon who oversees this joke of a prison camp."

"There's no need. I'm glad to have been of service."

"Well, I should like to demonstrate my appreciation. Come to my quarters for a drink tomorrow evening at seven o'clock."

"Thank you, sir," lied Kurt. He decided to risk Engel's wrath for declining. "Unfortunately, I have already made arrangements for tomorrow night."

"Arrangements?"

"Yes, to see an American girl I have met working."

"Of course. I wouldn't want to spoil your fun. I hear American girls are easy." Engel gave an ugly laugh. "You've earned the right to some pleasure. Some other time then. Goodnight, Brandt."

"Goodnight, sir."

Stressed, Kurt pushed his hand back through his hair after Engel had left. A drink in the officer's hut would be entering the lions' den yet again. He'd got away with it once. He wouldn't next time.

Kurt would have to run if Engel renewed the invitation. Dieter would need to run too. Abscond while they were at work.

Kurt decided that he could worry about it if it happened. Engel may not repeat his offer. Thinking of his forthcoming date with Jessie was much more satisfying. He couldn't let it be ruined by this. Lying in bed, he concentrated on imagining Jessie's face and kissing her once more. Try as he might an image of Hofmann blocked her out, the man demanding that Kurt be executed for desertion.

The next evening, Jessie brought her father's truck and drove them into town.

"I thought I'd take you to a diner for an authentic American experience."

'Jerry's Diner' proclaimed a red neon sign against the pink and purples streaks of the twilight Texan sky. On the door hung a sign, 'Whites only'. Inside, the interior of a long chrome counter behind which food was prepared and the red-topped stools were a wonder to Kurt. It was like arriving in the future. They sat down opposite each other at a table by one of the large windows.

"Do you like it?" asked Jessie.

"I love it."

"Check out the menu and choose what you want."

"I'm not that hungry," he fibbed. "You go ahead."

"It's okay, Kurt. I know you guys don't get paid with greenbacks. This is my treat. Don't feel bad, just enjoy it."

Kurt salivated as he examined the choices. A woman in a red dress matching the decor arrived.

"You guys ready to order?"

"Yes. Can I get the cheeseburger and fries."

"Me too," said Kurt.

Afterwards, they shared the largest ice cream sundae that Kurt had ever seen, covered in a generous helping of chocolate sauce. Kurt's face was pure sunshine.

"You might want to wipe your mouth," laughed Jessie. "There's a lot of chocolate on it." Blushing, Kurt did so. "Shall we choose something on the jukebox?"

She led him to the corner where a machine stood that looked to him as if it had landed from outer space. It was illuminated, decorated in a garish lime green and dark pink.

"Never used one before?" asked Jessie, observing the look of fascination on his face. She dropped a coin in the machine. "You choose the record you want and it'll play it for us. How about some Glen Miller?"

She pressed some of the lighted buttons set out beneath a stack of records visible through the glass. The turntable to the side of them rose. One of the records moved sideways onto it, and the turntable rose a little higher to reach the needle which dropped onto the record. The optimistic, carefree sound of 'In the Mood' erupted from the speaker.

"Pretty neat, don't you think?"

"Incredible." Kurt was completely sold.

When the music ended, they left. Jessie drove them out of town but not in the direction of the camp. They bumped along a dirt track into forest, coming to a halt by a lake. The reflection of a yellow moon slowly danced on its surface. Jessie's perfume and the scent of the pines added to the enchantment of the spot. Kurt was having the time of his life.

"Let's go for a swim," she said as she got out of the vehicle. In an instant, she had kicked off her shoes and slipped out of her dress. Kurt gawked. "Come on, don't just stand there."

Fumbling with his buttons, Kurt also undressed to his underwear and hurried into the lake to join her, forgetting for once his fear of water. He waded in as Jessie swam off. Once he reached waist height, he came to a halt.

"I can't swim."

Jessie swam back. Reaching Kurt, she threw her arms around him, pressing her lips to his. Kurt sank into her embrace, his body tingling from head to toe. A powerful feeling of desire which was growing stronger by the second consumed his whole being. Suddenly, Jessie broke away.

"I better get you back."

She moved towards the shore. Confused and disappointed, Kurt remained where he was for a while. He didn't understand why she had stopped. He was on fire and she had left him to burn. Kurt wondered if she had the same feelings for him that he had for her, or whether he was just a temporary amusement. Merely a placeholder until the local boys came home when the fighting ended.

Neither spoke on the journey back to the camp. An unexpected awkwardness occupied the space between them.

"See you tomorrow," said Jessie as she dropped him off.

Absorbed by his own thoughts of disillusionment, Kurt wandered slowly through the shadows back to his hut. When a hand was placed firmly over his mouth and he was put in an arm lock, it was totally unexpected.

CHAPTER 20

Kurt couldn't see them as he was manoeuvred forwards, almost bent double. They steered him towards a hut at the far end of the compound. The officers' hut.

Shoved through the door, he entered the room that he had once before. Three men sat behind a table. One he recognised but didn't know his name. He knew the names of the other two. Engel and Hofmann. A figure who stood facing them, turned his head, his face contorted with fear. It was Dieter. With an aggressive push from behind, Kurt was positioned next to him.

"Ziegler and Schmidt," began Engel in an imperious manner. "Stammführer Hofmann has explained to us how you both ran away from a Kinderlandverschickung to avoid having to fight the enemy. You have betrayed the Führer and the Fatherland, and failed in your duty to defend them. You probably thought that you'd got away with it. Lying to me that you'd left your homes to fight before being captured in France, and adopting new names. But you forget that in the

Reich the truth will always out, and justice will always prevail.

"You are both charged with the crime of desertion. Do you have anything that you wish to say before sentence is passed?" Dieter who had spent the whole time since Kurt had arrived with his head bowed shook his head. "Ziegler?"

"Yes, I do," said Kurt with defiance. "Have you asked Stammführer Hofmann how it is that he came to be a prisoner of the Americans when he was supposed to be hundreds of kilometres away fighting the Russians? He was happy to send us off to die on the Eastern Front but unwilling to lead by example it would seem."

Hofmann leapt to his feet, his anger apparent from the puce colour rapidly infusing his cheeks and the small droplets of spit flying from his mouth like bullets as he ranted.

"How dare you question my honour! I was commanded to assist the Hitler Youth panzer division on the Western Front. Young men who were willing to die for their country, not miserable cowards like you two."

"We have heard quite enough from you, Ziegler," said Engel. He conferred only briefly with Hofmann and the other officer. "It is abundantly clear that you two deserted your posts. There is only one possible sentence. Death."

He pronounced the word with a grim relish. Although he fought not to show it, Kurt's legs had turned to mush. Next to him, Dieter was visibly trembling.

"The sentence will be carried out tomorrow morning when the others have departed for work. I will arrange for someone to answer for you at roll call. The Americans are very sloppy. They assume that because someone answers to their name that they are present. Hauptmann and Ulbricht," he said looking at the two guards who had brought Kurt in, "you will keep them here tonight and escort them back to their hut tomorrow morning when the men go outside. Make sure the Americans don't see you moving them, and ensure that these two don't leave their hut under any circumstances before we arrive to dispense justice. Heil Hitler."

The officers rose and retired.

"Sit against the wall," commanded the man who Engel had addressed as Hauptmann. "And no talking."

Kurt fought not to retch as he considered their fate. It would be just like Kessel. A hanging presented as a suicide. Yet that would look like too much of a coincidence, and even more so that there should be two of them. No, it would have to be something else. Suffocation maybe. That could be blamed on the others in the hut, leaving someone else to take the fall if the Americans investigated. More probably, it would remain an unsolved murder. After all, what did they count for? Germans killed by other Germans. Why should their captors even care? It would be two less mouths for them to feed.

He thought of Jessie. Kurt would never get to tell her that he loved her, never get to know if she felt the same way. Tears welled up in his eyes, some escaping and running down his face. Life just wasn't fair. Why had this happened after they had cheated death and escaped undetected right across Nazi Germany, and when an end to fighting and freedom was so close that he could almost reach out and touch it? How ironic that his mother had sent him away to the country to be safe. In all likelihood if he had remained in London, he would have survived unscathed. Now she would never know his true fate. He would die alone, his story untold.

At some point, snoring next to him told him that Dieter had succumbed to sleep. Kurt must have also because it was a slap on the face which woke him from his slumber. With their arms pinned up against their backs once more, they were steered behind the huts and into theirs. Everyone had already left for morning roll call.

"Go lie down and don't move."

They retreated to the back corner where their beds were located. Kurt climbed up onto the top bunk. He thought he could hear Dieter snivelling intermittently in the bed beneath. Poor Dieter, his faithful friend. He should have left him at the monastery. His death in battle would have been swift. Not the prolonged torment that he had endured since yesterday. So many hours of waiting, waiting for the inevitable.

Shafts of early morning sun came through the small windows up high. Out there it was a beautiful day. Men were chatting and laughing. In here, separated from life by only wooden planks, they were cut off, trapped and helpless, like cattle awaiting slaughter. They would hear the trucks depart and all would be quiet. Then the door would open, and in would stride Hofmann and Engel, righteous and triumphant.

Kurt could put up a fight but they and their two helpers would be able to pin him down, killing him and his friend. Then the officers would leave, unaccountable, and never to be punished. Hofmann had brutalised so many adolescents, and sent so many off to fight, not caring that they would die. Murdering Kurt and his friend would mean nothing to him, nothing more than swatting a fly. A man without qualms. Engel was of the same ilk. Amoral men, willing henchmen of an evil regime.

Kurt turned onto his side and faced the wall, curling up with his hands between his knees. He'd lost the will to resist. It was pointless. It was over.

The door opened and footsteps echoed off the floor. Kurt couldn't bring himself to look. Below him, Dieter was now sobbing.

"Hey, I hear there's two sick in here."

The words weren't spoken in German and the voice was bright and breezy. Kurt couldn't believe his own ears. It wasn't their would be killers. Who had reported them as sick to save them he didn't know, but it was a miracle. He jumped down from the bed.

"We're feeling better now, sir. Ready to work."

"Well, you better hurry, the trucks are just leaving."

"Come on, Dieter."

They ran out into the sunshine. Engel's guards could do nothing. As Kurt looked to his right, he saw Hofmann and Engel stop in their tracks as they emerged from their quarters. He couldn't discern their expressions from this distance, but he grinned as he imagined their indignant incandescence at having been thwarted.

Never had it felt so good to be outside. He and Dieter jumped onto the back of the truck only seconds before it began moving. Kurt flung his head back in relief, before bringing it slowly forward again. His smile had died. This was only a temporary reprieve. Nothing had really changed. Tonight when they returned, the executioners would be waiting.

They couldn't go back to the camp. Kurt shared his thoughts with Dieter.

"We've got to run. It's our only chance."

Kurt thought again of Jessie. Today might be the last time that he ever saw her. Should he say something? He still hadn't made up his mind when he joined the line for lunch. But she wasn't there. Was it because of last night? It seemed that he would never know.

Come the afternoon, Kurt and Dieter worked a patch of land on the edge of the plantation. When all had their backs to them, they made their move. Crossing neighbouring farmland and bypassing the town of Huntsville, Kurt led them to the forest which only the previous evening he had visited with Jessie under very different circumstances.

"We'll hide here until it gets dark, and then go find a train to hitch a ride on. Get far away, like we did last time."

"But there's no front line to aim for. We can't escape from America, it's too big."

"We don't need to. We can find work somewhere, disappear into one of the big cities. Find a job and lie low until the war ends, and then - well, I think I might stay. You could too if you want. I'll teach you to speak English. They won't even know that we've escaped once we find some clothes to replace these ones."

Kurt's cloud had a silver lining. He could write to Jessie and tell her his story. And one day come back for her. Everything was going to work out.

That night, they hiked back to town with a swagger in their step, and climbed aboard an empty goods wagon which was already hitched to a locomotive. In the morning, their new adventure would begin. No longer children, and no longer conscripted soldiers or prisoners of war, they could write their own future. An exciting one where the claws of the past couldn't reach them. They would set off across this vast land, foot loose and fancy free.

Kurt and Dieter didn't get very far. In fact, they didn't get anywhere at all. Shortly after the sun rose, they were discovered by a couple of railway employees. In less than an hour, the young men were back at the camp.

CHAPTER 21

"You boys are in serious trouble. Why'd you do it? Don't you realise how well you're treated here? Uncle Sam bends over backwards for you guys. We're meticulous in observing the Geneva Convention. You eat better than most of the country do. Many folks are up in arms about it, especially now they're getting to hear about what Hitler's been up to."

The commander was as stern-faced as a battleship. His expression only relaxed when Kurt explained their reason for running. "I thought we'd already weeded out the die-hard Nazis. Well, you don't need worry no more. We have a special camp in Oklahoma for their kind."

Later that day, Engel, Hofmann, and their helpers were driven away. It had been a good day after all. Kurt's dreams were still alive. And tonight was movie night.

But it was no ordinary movie night. The entire camp was made to attend. On the screen, pictures appeared of emaciated individuals whose eyes were devoid of emotion, watching from behind barbed wire fences as American soldiers entered their concentration camp. The footage switched to naked, skeletal bodies piled upon one another. Those attending expressed profound shock and surprise. Kurt questioned if it really could be the case that the average German had no idea of what had been perpetrated in their name for so long on so many.

The newsreel haunted Kurt. It wouldn't let him sleep. He thought of Karolina. Recaptured, she must surely be dead. Her body discarded as casually as a cigarette butt, thrown onto such a heap of corpses if she hadn't already been killed while she lay in the long grass by the pear trees patiently awaiting rescue. Dead. Dead because of him.

He could have ignored her protest, but Kurt had taken the easy way out. He was complicit in her death because it had been easier to go along with what she wanted, what she had pretended that she wanted. She was the brave one, not him. He had been a coward. Just as Hofmann, who he so despised, had fled to save his own skin so had Kurt, abandoning Karolina in her hour of greatest need. Others might not know what Kurt had done but he did. Even when he regained his liberty, his freedom wouldn't be complete. Kurt could never be really free while he kept the truth a prisoner.

The next day a storm rolled in. As the prisoners stood to attention in the downpour with lightning attacking the sky like artillery fire, the camp commander addressed them.

"Yesterday the German High Command surrendered unconditionally to Allied forces. The war in Europe is over."

Many cheered at the news. Imprisonment would end and they could return home to resume some kind of normal life. Dieter was happy.

"I'll get to go back to Hamburg and see my mother. And my sister too. Our nightmare is at an end."

Noticing that his friend didn't seem equally pleased, he asked Kurt what he would do.

"I'll try to get back to England, I suppose." Although that was what he said, it wasn't what he was hoping for. More than anything, he wanted to stay here in Texas. A life in the sun, in a country which seemed full of possibility. He would ask Jessie at lunch break if she knew how he might go about it in a legal way.

However, yet again she wasn't there. Back at camp, he and the others who worked at the plantation were told that the owner would no longer be requiring their services and that they would be found an alternative place of work. Kurt was perplexed. Something must have happened, but he couldn't work out what that could be. Perhaps it was to do with the news of the atrocities at the concentration camps. He could see why that would have turned people against them, making them pariahs to be shunned.

Kurt had to go and see her, talk to her. Explain that

he was no part of it, that he was innocent. Finally, tell her the truth.

Managing to obtain a pass the next day, he walked the few miles to the ranch house. It was late in the afternoon when he got there. Jessie was sitting in a rocking chair. When she saw him, she came down from the verandah. The skin on her face had a sallow tint to it. She wasn't wearing makeup, and looked as if she hadn't slept well the night before.

"What are you doing here?" The usual welcome in her voice was absent.

"I wanted to see you. Now that the war's over, we'll be freed soon. I want to stay. Stay in America." Kurt decided to cast off the fear which held him back. "Jessie, I love you."

As he put his arms out to embrace her, she looked horrified at the prospect and moved back.

"It can't happen, you and me. Never."

"Why? I thought you liked me. What have I done?"

"We got news the other day that my brother was killed fighting in Germany. Daddy's beside himself. I can't be with you, a German. It would crush him. I'm the only family that he has left. You need to go."

"But Jessie, I'm not German, I'm English. My father's German. He abandoned us when I was a boy. I was evacuated out of London. My landlady was working for the Nazis, helping a spy. He kidnapped me and took me to Germany. They wanted me to fight for them so I ran away to the frontline and surrendered."

His explanation did nothing to change her demeanour. On the contrary, it made her angry.

"Stop! Just stop, will you. Don't you know how ridiculous you sound? I don't want to listen to your lies. Now go."

"But-"

"Go." She advanced and shoved him away with her arm.

Her look was implacable. Turning her back on him, she went inside the house. Moments later, she reappeared holding a rifle.

"I said go, get off our property. And don't ever come back."

Reeling from the rejection, Kurt departed. Once again, he was down in the dirt, mud in his mouth.

Days became weeks, which became months, months of monotony. Sleep, work, repeat. Rules were relaxed and passes to visit town easily obtained, but Kurt didn't go there. There was no point. What he thought that he once had, had vanished, consumed by the insanity of war.

Freedom didn't come as quickly as expected. When Kurt turned eighteen, they were still POWs. Then rumours began spreading that they would soon be on their way. Nearly two years after their arrival, Kurt and Dieter found themselves on the train again, travelling North this time.

Kurt had accepted that he would be returning to Germany. He hadn't attempted to tell anyone else of his past. If even Jessie thought that he was lying, what chance was there of a stranger believing his account? Once back in Germany, he could find a way back to England. After all, he'd made it from Poland to France during wartime. By comparison, this time it should be easy. He could walk to the coast and stowaway on a boat if need be.

Watching the American coastline fade from view as he stood on the deck of the troop carrier assigned to transport the POWs, Kurt was deep in the doldrums. His dream of staying, dream of marrying Jessie, those dreams were long gone but it still hurt. Loneliness had returned as his closest acquaintance and refused to budge from his side.

Once out at sea, they were given the news withheld from them on land. They weren't going to Germany. Britain, which was short of workers, needed them. They were to remain POWs. No duration was specified.

CHAPTER 22

All save Kurt were downhearted. Excitement at seeing family again was replaced by frustration at the prospect of yet more years away from home and loved ones.

When the ship sailed into Liverpool, grey and dismal under a low roof of unbroken clouds, the scene which greeted them reminded Kurt of London. Piles of rubble and vacant lots occupied large swathes of the city. As they were marched to the station, some of those watching their procession jeered. The memories of war were still raw and bitter.

Transferred by train to Newcastle in the North East, they were made to walk ten miles through unrelenting rain to 'Camp 69' on the outskirts of the small town of Ponteland. Their soggy clothes stuck to them like tape. It could not have been a bigger contrast to the soporific heat of Texas.

The helpings of food were small, and the meals even worse than Kurt had remembered. There were no movie nights under the stars, no movies at all. Sent out to surrounding farms, the POWs worked in the fields. They sank their heads below their shoulders in a futile attempt to avoid the bite of the wind, which never seemed to cease blowing across this wild and open country stretching towards Hadrian's wall and Scotland. No wonder, thought Kurt, that Roman soldiers had regarded a posting here as one of the worst in the whole Roman Empire.

Early in the new year, Kurt requested a meeting with the officer in charge of the camp. Now that he was back in England, he would try once more. The man displayed an incredulous scepticism like those who Kurt had previously told. Desperate to get out, he persevered this time.

"Sir, could you please at least write to my mother to seek corroboration."

"Most mothers that I know will say anything to help a son."

"Then could you not make enquiries of the authorities to establish that I'm telling the truth, that I was evacuated to Dulverton and disappeared without trace? Surely if that is confirmed, you must believe me. How could a thirteen year old boy possibly have got to Germany from there of his own volition?"

The man leaned back in his chair and put his arms behind his head as he considered Kurt's argument.

"I would be inclined to agree with you there. Leave it with me. Meanwhile, I'm obliged to continue to treat you as a prisoner of war. I should hear back within a couple of weeks. If it is as you say, you will be released."

"Thank you, sir. I really do appreciate it."

Kurt's hopes of an early resolution were dashed by 1947 being Britain's worst winter of the twentieth century. Snow fell day after day until it was so deep that drifts were as high as houses.

The country ground to a halt for several weeks, beaten not by Germany but by nature.

Called upon to assist in the relief effort, the men carried coal and other supplies through blizzards to those cut off. Kurt had never experienced weather like it. It was as if the Ice Age had returned with a vengeance. The camp huts, which had always been damp and never warm, became human fridges. Everyone went to bed fully clothed, yet even wearing the coats and woolly hats that they had been issued with couldn't insulate them from the bitterly cold air. Pipes froze and no one could wash.

It was a miserable existence, not just for them but for an entire country which had already been brought to its knees after years of war. Britain may have won the moral victory, standing alone against Hitler as a beacon of hope and freedom to an enslaved Europe until Russia and America had joined the war, which had enabled the madman to be beaten. But Britain's fight had cost it everything that it had. Its coffers were empty, and the money which America had loaned it would need to be repaid, every single cent of it. Though some might not appreciate it yet, the sun was already setting on the British Empire. Britain's days as a world power were fast drawing to a close.

It wasn't until nearly April that the snowfalls ended, and with the disruption it was already May when Kurt was summoned. His stomach turned over as he entered the room. In that quintessentially British fashion, the man began with an apology, usually a precursor of bad news.

"Sorry about the delay. But as you can imagine the government's had more pressing issues to deal with recently. I only received a response yesterday. Anyway, you'll be pleased to hear that your account has been confirmed so I am able to release you immediately."

Kurt's shoulders subsided in relief. At last, after six years he would be free to get on with his life.

"Excellent. Thank you, sir." He shook the man's offered hand energetically.

"I'm sorry you've had to endure all that you have. Still, look on the bright side. You could write a book about it. I'm sure it'd be a best seller. We'll issue you with some civilian clothes, and money to get you home."

Home. The word had a hollow ring to it. Being a POW had at least brought some security and stability to his life. London had been his home once. However, with the family house gone, he no longer had a place to call home. His mother's husband was as unlikely to want him now as before, yet he had nowhere else to go.

Before he left, Kurt waited for Dieter to return from the fields. His jaw opened like a chasm when he saw his friend in a suit and hat.

"I'm happy for you." But the words fell from his mouth with a poorly concealed sadness.

"I'll write to you once I get settled, and be sure to keep in touch when you get back to Germany." Both young men felt awkward in the suppressed emotion of the moment. For a large part of their lives, circumstance had thrown them together. A strong bond forged in hardship and danger. Now they would go their separate ways and probably never meet again. Kurt thought about hugging his friend but didn't. "Well, I must be off or I'll miss my train."

Wanting to preserve the limited money which he had, Kurt spent the night sitting in the waiting room at Newcastle station. It was no great hardship for one who was rejuvenated by the happiness of being released, and a lot warmer than the nights spent in bed at the camp that winter. Arriving in London, his feelings were a whirlpool of conflicting emotions. Although eager to see his mother, the wound of rejection which had never fully healed was weeping again.

Like Liverpool, London was cut and scarred. Although the Blitz had ended early in the war, during the last two years of it the city had been under heavy attack again. This time from thousands of rockets fired from German bases in France and Holland. Early versions were nicknamed buzz-bombs or doodlebugs. They sounded like old motor bikes whizzing across the sky. Later ones were silent, arriving without warning and giving those on the receiving end no time to take evasive action.

Before seeking out Bill's road, Kurt went to his old street. It seemed to whisper his name, but he wasn't sure if it was in greeting or mockery. Several houses, his included, had disappeared. Empty spaces where once there had been life. Childhood memories ran down the street towards him but he didn't linger. He wanted to see his mother. Finding Bill's house, he knocked.

"Hello, it's me Kurt."

"What are you doing here?" Bill's face was a dark cloud.

"I've come to see mum."

"You're too late for that."

"Late?"

"She passed away last year."

Kurt swayed involuntarily with shock.

"How?"

"The doctor said it was a heart attack, probably caused by a congenital condition. But I blame you. It broke her heart, you running away, just disappearing like that. You have no idea the upset that you caused. It destroyed her, not knowing where you were, if you were alive or dead. And you didn't even have the decency to send a letter to let her know that you were all right. You disgust me. Don't ever darken my door again."

He left Kurt facing a closed door.

CHAPTER 23

Kurt couldn't hold back the tears as he went down the street. Passers-by looked the other way. Grief was something to be kept under lock and key, only to be let out in the privacy of one's own home. Public displays of emotion were undignified, not British.

He found a hostel to spend the night, not that he could sleep. In captivity, he'd often imagined going home when the war ended, the joy on his mother's face as she opened the door, and how good it would be to see her again. Now that wasn't going to happen. Never. The fury which he had often felt when he thought of Miss Althorpe reached a new level of intensity, one that he couldn't ignore.

Kurt made a plan. When he had earned some money, he would take a trip down to Dulverton, and confront her before going to the police. He wanted to see the disbelief on her face, savour that moment when she discovered that she hadn't got away with it and realised that she would pay for her treachery, and pay for all that she had done to an innocent child.

Kurt secured a job in a warehouse. With his first wage, he bought a ticket to Dulverton. The countryside in early June looked bountiful, the desolation of a harsh winter already forgotten. Hedgerows sung with the birds who had made their homes amongst them, and the air smelled of wild garlic as he walked along the road from the station. Kurt noticed none of this. Focused inward, the angry eyes of his mind had put up shutters against the world around him.

He banged aggressively on the front door, no longer the child forbidden to ever use it. She hadn't changed much, a few more silver streaks in her hair but still the same hostile persona that was her impenetrable suit of armour.

"Yes." The voice was as caustic as it had always been. Yet it wasn't one that indicated recognition.

"You don't know who I am do you?" Kurt fought to keep his tone calm and measured.

As Miss Althorpe took time to examine the man before her, the colour drained from her cheeks. She went to shut the door but he was quicker and stronger.

"Let's go in the lounge shall we," said Kurt after he had forced his way into the hallway. "Sit down on that chair. I want to know why you did it, why you betrayed your country."

"You wouldn't understand."

"Try me."

"It would be a waste of time."

"I've got an open mind," he lied. "I've come to listen."

For a moment it seemed she would maintain her refusal to talk, but then all of a sudden the words poured out of her as if she needed finally to justify her actions.

"I didn't betray this country. It was England that betrayed me, killed the only man who I ever loved. A man whose only crime was to love me back. My parents lived in India. I was brought up in Calcutta. I met a man in the army but my family didn't approve, none of the ruling class did. Amrit's skin wasn't the right colour. A wog, they called him. They tried everything to separate us, planned to send me back to England. So we ran away together. When they caught us they attacked him, beat him to death in front of me. Yes, that's him." Kurt was looking at the picture in the frame, the one which he had found as a boy.

"What happened made me realise the truth about the bloody British Empire. It's not the munificent force it portrays itself to be. It's a brutal occupying power which exploits people, making them hate each other. Divide and rule is their method of government, treating the inhabitants with contempt and little better than slaves.

"I wanted to play a role in ending it. When there was talk of war, I offered my services to the German embassy. If England lost, its Empire would collapse. India and the other colonies would become free at last. I would have done my bit in fighting evil, in avenging all the men, women and children that the Empire has treated no better than my Amrit.

"You probably think that I'm an unfeeling, cold-hearted harridan. Once I was very different, full of joy and hope for the future. It's what they did that made me who I am today."

The emotional damn holding back Kurt's anger burst.

"But what right did that give you to make me suffer? For years I have been a prisoner, first in a hellish place in Poland and then as a POW. My childhood lost, stolen because of you!"

His voice had risen to a shout.

"Yes, the circumstances were unfortunate. I'm sorry you had to go through that."

"Sorry? Well, sorry's not enough."

"Are you're going to tell the police?"

"Yes, why wouldn't I?"

"It won't change anything."

"I've heard enough."

Kurt stormed out of the house, slamming the door. However, as he walked down the hill, his rage began to subside. Maybe she was right. Was there any point informing the police? Would it really make him feel any better? He wasn't going to find happiness in revenge. Wrapping himself in hatred and bitterness wouldn't ever bring him joy. Miss Althorpe was a clear example of that.

A loud sound from inside the house, which made several crows take flight in a flutter of wings, decided the issue for him. The matter was already closed.

On the way back to the station, Kurt let himself absorb the calm and beauty of his surroundings. He had confronted that which had gnawed at him for so long and felt better for it. It was as if a tide had come in and washed away his torment at the loss of his youth. History couldn't be changed, but at long last he had his freedom. He needed to use it and find a life. Not waste it, forever locked in the prison cell of his past, acting as his own jailor.

Working in the warehouse didn't fulfil him. His days were spent in semi-darkness without stimulation or satisfaction, and London had lost any charm it might once have held for him. Kurt was but another anonymous soul, an unknown face in the crowds. When autumn came and pea soup fogs fed by a forest of chimneys descended for days on end, creating a ghostly world where people suddenly appeared and then just as quickly disappeared back into the sickly smog, he decided to choose change.

Returning to Dulverton, he found a room to rent at the Boot, a cottage just two doors up from the pub, and secured a job at the bookshop. Down here, the fog was natural and beguiling. Autumn mists rose like stage curtains made of steam to reveal hills of gold as the sun reflected off a million yellow leaves. Now old enough to enter the Bridge Inn, he enjoyed a visit there on his first Saturday afternoon. Cosy and comfortable sitting by the roaring fire, he read the newspaper. When he went up for his second beer, the man behind the bar looked at him as he poured his drink.

"I knew you looked familiar. You're that Kurt chap, aren't you? The one that ran away."

"Guilty."

"I thought as much."

"I moved back. I'm working in the bookshop."

"Well I never."

Word soon spread. Many locals came to the shop, not with the intention of buying a book but curious to set eyes on him once again. Mrs Bishop was among them.

"I'm so happy to know that you're safe. You had us all worried when you disappeared. Where on earth did you go?"

Kurt gave her the same answer which he had to everyone else who had asked.

"Away. I don't really want to talk about it. It all turned out right in the end, and I'm glad to be back."

"I blamed myself for placing you with Miss Althorpe. She wasn't the most Christian of women. Still, we shouldn't speak ill of the dead. The poor woman killed herself not long ago. She must have been so unhappy to do an awful thing like that. Always insisted on keeping herself to herself she did. I doubt she would have accepted help even if we had appreciated the state she was in." Kurt made no comment. "Well, I do hope that we might see you in church."

This time he did go, and he joined the choir. Kurt was part of a community that he wanted to belong to for the first time in his life. Going to the pub with the others after rehearsals was the part which he enjoyed most. Walking home afterwards, he would be smiling to himself, refreshed after an evening of company and laughter.

Kurt thought often of Jessie but knew that it was pointless. He would never see or hear from her again. Eventually, his thoughts turned to Barb. Early one Sunday with a thick frost crunching beneath his feet and the sun not yet above the treetops, he walked along the river towards the farm.

The house was no longer on the verge of dereliction. It had been painted white, and had a new door of olive green. Tentatively, he knocked on the door, almost wishing that he hadn't and tempted to run. A middle-aged lady with ginger hair and rosy cheeks opened it.

"Sorry to bother you. I was passing by and was wondering if Barb still lived here. I'm an old friend."

"No my dear, she had to leave when her father died. Me and my husband, we bought the farm off the bank. I think she moved off up to Exmoor, or the coast, summat like that."

"Oh."

"Goodbye then."
After that, Kurt put Barb to the back of his mind as he had tried to do with Jessie.

CHAPTER 24

Amongst the maze of wooden shelves of books, many of which had probably been there well before he had arrived in the town as an evacuee, and the all pervasive musty smell of his workplace, Kurt began to wonder if he really could write a book as the officer in Northumberland had suggested. On a day off, he took the bus to Tiverton, and came home with what he wanted. It was heavy and black with the manufacturer's name in gold letters.

In his room, he placed the typewriter on the small table by the window overlooking the high street, and stood back to admire his new possession. The keys were circular, some of the letters faded from use. Kurt sat down, fed a sheet of paper into the machine and began typing with two fingers. He stopped to examine his work, only three words in total: 'An Evacuee's Story'.

What to write next proved to be too much of a challenge. Writing a whole book seemed impossible, a gargantuan task that was beyond him. Kurt left the paper sitting untouched in the machine. It had been a stupid idea. He wasn't a writer.

One evening over a week later, he forced himself to sit down in front of the machine, still not knowing what to write. Yet inexplicably this time the words came, flowing out of him like a sinner eager to confess, the ink hitting the paper fast and furiously. That night he stayed up until gone two o'clock. Kurt found it cathartic to let it all out at last, and not hide his past as he had chosen to do in the real world.

The long dark evenings of that winter passed in a flash, so absorbed had Kurt become in his writing. Come spring, he had finished. Over two hundred neatly stacked pages sat next to his typewriter. It wasn't Shakespeare or Dickens, but it came from the heart. The East End boy who had gone half way around the world and back again.

In the shop during the long periods between customers, Kurt read a book on how to get published. Following the advice which it contained, he wrote a synopsis and retyped the first chapter a few times, posting the material to publishers in London and then waited. Summer came. There were no replies, not even an acknowledgement. Fame and fortune it seemed were not to be his destiny.

Now that it was no longer a restricted area, Kurt decided to venture up onto Exmoor for the first time. The bus followed the narrow winding road as it climbed through broadleaf forest, a precipitous drop to the left hand side. Far beneath, a stream dropped over boulders through a narrow wooded valley with no trace of human intervention. A secret, untouched world. Then, without warning, they broke through the tree cover and into an altogether different landscape.

Kurt got off and began walking. The view from up here seemed endless. High rolling moorland punctuated only by a thin ribbon of road and blanketed in a carpet of purple heather. Life affirming bird song came from somewhere up high. There was nothing and no one, nothing but him and a soft breeze under a sapphire sky.

Exhilarated by his surroundings, he followed a track, feeling freer than he had at any time since he was a young child. Eventually, the path dipped into a valley where sheep sat munching on the grass, their jaws moving lethargically from side to side as they observed him pass. Below him, he spied a few dwellings and the welcome sight of wooden tables and benches outside one of them. Reaching the pub, he went in to order a ginger beer and a ploughman's lunch before sitting down outside in the warm sunshine.

"There you go." The waitress placed a plate containing a thick slice of bread, a hunk of cheddar cheese, a slice of ham, and pickles on the table. "Can I get you anything else?"

Kurt looked up intending to smile and say no thank you. Time stopped.

"Barb?"

She moved back, as if not knowing what to make of this stranger who knew her by a name which she no longer used.

"You must have me confused with someone else." He stood and removed his sun hat.

"It's me. Kurt." Immobile as though he had turned her to stone, she said nothing. "It is you, isn't it?"

She looked around her to see if anyone was listening to them, but the others were all too busy chatting and enjoying their drinks to notice.

"I can't talk, I've work to do."

"You must be closing for the afternoon soon. I'll wait here."

"I…"

"I only want to talk to you. Please. For old time's sake."

"All right then, but not here. I'll see you down by the river at the end of the lane in half an hour."

She hurried back inside. It was almost an hour until she arrived. Traces of the girl he remembered remained but there was something different about her, something much more than her freckles having disappeared.

"It's lovely to see you, Barb. How are you?"

"I'm fine. I'm glad to know that you're all right. No one knew where you went to."

"Well, I'm back now working in the bookshop in Dulverton. Do you live here?"

"No, on the coast. I have a couple of bar jobs. In my spare time, I help out with the ponies. There were only fifty of them left by the end of the war. Shot by soldiers or killed by people for meat. It's desperately sad. I'll never understand how we can hurt defenceless animals. They don't have a wicked bone in their body, not like humans. I must be going or I'll miss my bus."

"Did you fancy meeting up for a drink sometime?"

"I can't."

"Is there someone else?"

"No."

"Don't you like me then?"

"No, it's not that. I like you a lot, I always have. Look, I can't explain, and it's best that you don't ask. Please try to understand. If you like me at all, you'll leave me alone and let me be. I really have to go."

Baffled, Kurt watched her head back up the hill as she waved furiously at the bus to wait for her. Of the two women Kurt had cared about apart from his mother, one thought he was a liar and the other wouldn't tell him the truth. Despite the uplifting otherworldliness of Exmoor, Kurt felt glum as he began the long walk back.

His low mood lifted the next day when a letter arrived from a publisher in London expressing interest and suggesting a meeting. Taking a day off from work, Kurt took the train up with his entire manuscript, holding it close as if it was his newborn baby.

"It'll need quite a bit of editing, but I think you could have something here," said the man he met who went by the name of Chuck, an enthusiastic American. "Leave it with me. When I've read it all, I'll discuss it with my editorial board and be in touch. By the way, who is it dedicated to? Every book must have a dedication."

Kurt didn't need to think. "Karolina."

Kurt was excited as he travelled back. Maybe this would be it, a book deal.

In the weeks which followed, he often thought about Barb and what could possibly have happened to make her as she was. Kurt decided to ask Mavis Robinson, a lady in the choir, who appeared to be the repository for all local gossip, and not adverse to sharing it with whoever would listen.

"Word is she had a baby, and that's why she stopped going to school. They say the child was taken away from her."

"What about the father? Wouldn't he marry her?"

"That was the problem. She was never seen with anyone, apart from yourself that is."

"Well, I can assure you that it wasn't me," said Kurt affronted at the apparent implication.

"No one thought it was, or any other young lad for that matter."

"What do you mean?" His forehead creased in confusion.

She leaned towards him and lowered her voice.

"There were rumours."

"Rumours?"

"About her father. That he mistreated her, if you get my drift. I'll say no more."

Mavis placed a conspiratorial finger to her lips and went off to talk to another chorister. Kurt was too shocked to move. Such a thought had never crossed his mind. However, as he lay in bed that night, memories came flooding back. The black eye which she had blamed on her horse, the unpleasantness of the man when Kurt had encountered him that once, and how she appeared to live in permanent fear of her father. Poor Barb, how she must have suffered, alone and frightened. No one to confide in, no one to protect her.

On Sunday, he went back to the pub on Exmoor. This time he didn't go in but waited down the lane near the bus stop. At closing time, Barb appeared, walking down the lane. She came to an abrupt halt when she saw Kurt.

"I know what happened," he blurted out, "and I wanted you to know that it doesn't change how I feel about you. Not one bit."

"Well, that's good to know." The blood rushed to her cheeks. "You really don't get it, do you. It's changed me, changed how I feel. I don't want a relationship with you or anyone. I asked you to leave me be. Please respect that and don't ever bother me again."

She walked swiftly away from him. Kurt could do nothing but stand there. That wasn't the reaction he had expected, yet he could see it was a lost cause.

CHAPTER 25

Later that year, news came that Kurt's book was to be published. He received a substantial advance, enabling him to make an offer on a small cottage in Millham Lane. It was at the end of a row of identical houses. There was a small front garden entered through a wooden gate and the front door had a brass knocker in the shape of a fox's face. Inside it was small but cosy.

Mavis buttonholed him after choir.

"I hear you're buying a place."

"Who told you that?"

"It's a small town. Well, are you?"

"Yes, I am in fact."

"All I can say is that they must pay well in the bookshop."

Kurt didn't take the bait and moved away, leaving her burning with curiosity.

Life was perfect, almost. Kurt had a nice home, was financially comfortable, and part of a community. But there was one hole, a gaping hole. One that had been there for so long. He remained lonely and unloved. In bed at night, staring into the void of darkness engulfing him, he wondered if this was to be his forever destiny, to live a solitary existence. That Barb had rejected him no longer bothered him. It was for the best, he didn't truly love her. The only girl he did, he would never see again. Maybe one day someone else would steal his heart and he would forget about Jessie. Or maybe no one else ever would. But it seemed wrong to Kurt to settle, to spend his life with someone just for the sake of not being alone.

Invited to the book launch in London, Kurt was staggered to see how many people had turned up to the event. Through the haze of cigarette smoke, he observed the city crowd. It was a world away from his simple country life. The men were in dinner jackets, the ladies in evening gowns. Britain's grinding post-war austerity was something which they had evidently managed to dodge.

"Kurt!" His editor slapped him on the back and handed him a copy of the book taken from the display table. "What do you think of this then?"

Kurt could hardly believe his eyes. There, in bold letters, was his name on the cover.

"It's amazing. Thank you so much."

"No, thank you, buddy. We're looking at a best seller. Orders are already piling in. I've got London's top book critics here tonight. This thing is gonna be huge. It wouldn't surprise me if we don't soon have an offer from one of the film studios. And the company absolutely loves me right now for finding you. I'd like to meet with you early in the New Year to talk about a book tour. Now, if you'll excuse me, I need to go rub shoulders with the movers and shakers. Got your speech ready?"

"Speech?" Kurt's stomach tightened. Not used to being the centre of attention, he didn't welcome the prospect. He much preferred being an anonymous author, hiding behind the parapets of the written word. Grabbing a glass of champagne from a passing waiter, he downed it in one in an effort to control his nerves.

Several of the guests came to congratulate Kurt, although he barely took in what they were saying. He was too preoccupied by the thought of having to talk in front of these people. All too soon, Chuck was tapping his glass and calling for quiet. After a few pleasantries, he introduced Kurt and offered him the floor.

"Er...thanks, everyone. I'm afraid that I'm a writer, not a speaker." The flash of reporters' cameras blinded him. It helped, reducing his anxiety. He could no longer see that sea of eager faces all intently fixed upon him. "I'd like to thank Chuck and his company for supporting me, and any of you that may decide to read my book."

He stopped talking, lost for words. People began shouting questions at him.

"Are you in touch with your father, Kurt?"

"No."

"How about Karolina," asked another. "Do you know where she is?"

"No, I'm afraid not."

Chuck had insisted on changing his written account so that it didn't mention him abandoning Karolina. It would undermine reader empathy for the story and harm sales, he'd said.

"And what about the people of Dulverton? Are they excited to be put on the map?"

"I doubt it'll bother them, they're not like that. It won't interest them." Kurt didn't divulge that he wouldn't be ordering any copies of the book for the shop. He hadn't shared his story with anyone in the town, and it was too late to do that now.

Kurt was relieved when he got back home. No one would shove a camera in his face, or ask for his autograph. He could blend into the background again. All he had ever wanted was to be ordinary and to be accepted, not to stand out in a crowd.

Locking the shop one Saturday afternoon, he called in at The Bridge Inn on the way home.

"The usual please, Mike."

The barman gave him a quizzical look as he pulled the pint.

"Someone was in here asking about you the other day."

"Me?"

"Yes, you. Or did it slip your mind that you're famous? Surely you can't have forgotten that you've written a best seller. He was a journalist from London. He left me a copy of your book, and a few more with others I dare say." Kurt felt his cheeks glow and not from the warmth of the log fire. "We don't take kindly to being misled, or to our town being criticised. Enjoy your drink."

The barman slammed the glass of beer firmly down on the counter and turned his back on Kurt, not apologising that he'd caused a substantial spillage. Sheepishly, Kurt carried his drink to a chair in the far corner. As he glanced up at the other drinkers, they looked away, talking to each other in low voices so that he couldn't hear, but he could guess who they were talking about. Finishing his beer quickly, Kurt retreated to his cottage and remained there for the rest of the weekend.

On Monday morning, Mavis stormed into the bookshop.

"I'd like to order a book."

"What is it? We might have it in stock already?"

"I don't think so, it's by a Kurt Ziegler. The Evacuee's Story."

"Er…"

"What were you thinking, Kurt? This isn't the way you keep friends."

She didn't wait for an answer. Most of the town closed him down. Shopkeepers no longer asked how he was, limiting conversation to what it was that he wished to buy.

Kurt was cross with himself for not having been

open. It was just like before when he'd been evacuated here, ignored and unwanted. However, this time he only had himself to blame.

Not many locals frequented the bookshop any longer but plenty of day trippers did. Several asked for the book which he didn't have, and if he knew where the author lived. He would shake his head. Kurt did the same when some asked if he knew which was the house that the traitor, Miss Althorpe, had lived in.

Kurt suspected that the same questions were being asked of others in the local pubs and shops, rubbing salt in the wound of those who felt let down by him.

One evening, he got home to find a note posted through his door. *Go home. You're not wanted here,* it read. But this was his home or the closest thing that he had ever had to one since he had been eleven years old.

As he hung up his coat, there was a knock at the door. Kurt sighed. Someone else come to berate him no doubt.

CHAPTER 26

Kurt opened the door.

"May I come in?" said a chirpy voice. It was Mrs Bishop. "I wanted to check that you were all right." With an outstretched arm and no words, Kurt directed her into the small lounge.

"You poor thing, I had no idea of what you'd been through. Not only in Germany, but here also. You showed remarkable fortitude. I'm not sure that most of us would have been able to endure what you did."

"That's kind of you to say so."

"Though I'm afraid you've rather thrown away the sympathy that people would have felt by hiding from them what happened to you."

"Yes, I regret that now."

"Well, it's no used crying over spilled milk. I dare say that it'll all blow over in time. Whenever anyone goes on to me about it, I remind them to show some compassion as Jesus would have wanted us to. To be honest, some of those who call themselves Christians in this town are falling short at the moment. Anyway, if you need me, you know where to find me."

"Thank you, I really appreciate that. Can I offer you a cup of tea?"

"That would be lovely but I have to run. Toodle pip." With a cheery wave she departed.

It came as a relief when Chuck confirmed there was to be a book tour. Even better, that it was to be one of America, and that he'd be gone for a whole six weeks. Time for those in Dulverton to become less annoyed with him and move on to the latest gossip.

"It won't be a vacation," his editor warned him. "Three or four cities a day, and lots of travelling. You need to practice becoming ambidextrous or your right hand will seize up with all those book signings. The New York Times has published a favourable review which has been syndicated across the nation, and your book is in high demand.

"We need to strike while the iron's hot. In Britain, they'll still be talking about the war in fifty years, but in America it'll have been forgotten in five. They don't dwell on the past over there, they're much more interested in the future."

Kurt soon discovered that Chuck hadn't been exaggerating when he'd said that it wouldn't be a holiday. Kurt barely got to see any more of New York than when he had arrived there as a POW. It was the same in other places too. Another day, another train, another hotel room. Soon Kurt had lost track of which day it was, and which city they were in. They didn't look a whole lot different to each other from the inside of taxi cabs and bookstores.

He rarely took much notice of who was buying his book. On automatic pilot most of the time, he would raise his head for the briefest of moments, trying to make his smile seem genuine for the umpteenth time that day as he handed buyers his book. Sometimes he even failed to look up.

On the day which Kurt would always remember, he had already been up since five in the morning. A recent glance at his watch had told him that it was nearly six in the evening. The long opening hours in the USA were something which Chuck had omitted to mention when selling the book tour to him.

"I hope you enjoy it," said Kurt passing over a signed copy. He couldn't believe how mundane that sounded, but they weren't hearing it hundreds of times a day as he was.

"I'm so sorry I didn't believe you."

The timbre was unique. Kurt looked up from the hand. As it registered he leapt up, flabbergasted.

"Jessie. Oh my gosh. Can you wait? I'll be done in an hour."

"No, I have to go. Take good care of yourself, Kurt."

The next customer was already impatiently holding out a copy of the book for signature.

"Can you tell me where we are?" asked Kurt.

"Houston," said the man.

"Is that far from Huntsville?"

"Less than a hundred miles, I guess. Can you sign my book now?"

Kurt hailed a cab as he left the bookstore. It was gone nine in the evening when it dropped him. He could see the silhouette of a figure rise from the rocking chair on the verandah as he walked towards the house.

Jessie descended the few steps. "I can't believe you came. I feel so awful, not trusting you. Can you ever forgive me?"

"There's nothing to forgive."

"Really?"

"Absolutely."

Jessies' eyes had become watery pools. She wiped her hand across them.

"Have you got time for a drink? I made some lemonade earlier."

Kurt went to tell the cab driver not to wait, and sat down while she went indoors to pour his drink. He could still hardly believe that he was back here, that fate had taken him in a circle.

"There you go," said Jessie handing him a glass. "Can I fix you something to eat?"

"No, thanks. I'm not hungry. How did you know - "

"I read about you in the newspaper, and found out that you were coming to Houston to do a book signing."

"I'm so glad you did. Hopefully, your father will

feel differently about me now."

"He passed a year back."

"I'm sorry."

"Yeah, I miss him. The place is mine now. How have you been?"

Their conversation continued effortlessly even though they hadn't seen each other in so long. It must have been almost midnight when Jessie made her suggestion.

"Hey, how about a trip to the lake for old time's sake?"

Jessie laid out a blanket this time. Her touch was even better than he remembered. They stayed until dawn found them entwined in each other's embrace, two souls renewed.

When the book tour ended, Kurt didn't return to Dulverton. He went back to Huntsville. Two weeks later, he decided to propose. They were sitting on the steps leading up to the verandah while an orange sun sank into the landscape like a planet disappearing into the earth in slow motion.

"Jessie, there's something I wanted to ask you."

"Yes?" Her playful tone and the way she tilted her head indicated she knew what the question would be and that his request would be well received.

"First, there's something you need to know about me. I'm not that heroic figure who you read about in the book. The editor made me change my account. You see when Dieter and I were in the orchard in France near the front line, Karolina told us to go on without her. She said she'd slow us down. We should have ignored her and carried her but we didn't. We abandoned her, and ran off to save ourselves."

"And you think she died?"

"Yes. We asked the American soldiers to go and get her. There was a battle raging. They wouldn't. And where she'd been hiding was a pile of rubble."

"Oh, that's so sad. After you'd all got so far."

"I know. If only I could go back and do it all again, not make the same mistake."

Jessie put her hand on his.

"You can't blame yourself. Karolina knew that it was the right thing to do. To give you and Dieter a better chance of making it. Maybe she lived. Have you ever tried to find her?"

"No."

"Well, we could make inquiries. Try the Red Cross."

"So it doesn't change how you feel about me?"

"No, Kurt, it doesn't. And my answer's yes," she said flinging her arms around him and kissing him.

Kurt had finally found home. All the emptiness inside which had lived in him like a parasite since he was a boy had gone.

He did contact the Red Cross and various authorities. None had any record of Karolina. Kurt's fears that she hadn't survived were confirmed.

CHAPTER 27

Jessie and Kurt had three children. It was a good life. Kurt was grateful for all that he had, so much more than he'd ever dared hope for, and so much more than he felt that he deserved.

Reading of the devastating flood in August 1952 when nine inches of rain fell on an already saturated Exmoor in a single night, Kurt sent a thousand dollar donation to the relief fund. An unstoppable wall of water had barrelled through Dulverton, reaching Kurt's own height by his old lodgings at The Boot. Mrs Bishop wrote to thank him, saying that what Kurt had done had been mentioned at Sunday service and been greeted with warm applause.

I always said the upset about your book would blow over. Well, I was almost right. The flood washed it away. Fortunately, no lives were lost here but sadly up on the coast at Lynmouth, over thirty people died, and hundreds were made homeless when the raging waters cut a swathe of destruction through that town, carrying away buildings as if they were mere twigs.

On a happier note, we had been told to prepare for

a film crew coming to Dulverton in September to do outdoor shots for the film that they're making of your book. Everybody was quite excited at the prospect, especially the possibility of being used as extras. Due to the flood, filming has now been postponed until the spring. When it finally happens, I'm sure it will give us something to talk about for years to come. I do hope you will come and see us one day.

Kurt never did go back to Dulverton. He never even went back to England. He wrote to Dieter in Germany once but didn't receive a reply.

Raising a family and working the plantation made the years pass quickly, too quickly. All too soon the kids were grown and Kurt was no longer young.

It was just before his sixtieth birthday that Kurt got the unwelcome news. After months of unexplained stomach pains, he finally gave in to Jessie and went to see the doctor. That led to a hospital visit and a scan. Stomach cancer, they said. Inoperable. Chemo would buy a year maybe, possibly two. Kurt declined. He didn't consider the debilitating side effects to be worth it. Jessie respected his wishes and asked him if there was anything he would like to do.

"No, I've had everything a man could ask for. A wonderful wife and three great kids. There's only one thing in my life which I've done that I truly regret."

"I know, honey. But you need to let it go. None of us can go back and change what we did. I've been planning a trip for your birthday if you still feel up to it."

"Sure. I want to keep on going until I no longer can. Where are you taking me?"

"LA. We can do Disney and Universal Studios. Be like kids again."

Kurt was bemused by her choice but didn't want to appear ungrateful so he hid his ambivalence. Despite not ever having wanted to go there, he found himself swept up in the escapism of the theme parks. It was like living a childhood that he had never had.

"I've got us tickets to a TV studio filming," said Jessie on their last night. "For one of your favourite shows, 'The hero next door'."

Kurt held Jessie's hand as they sat watching uplifting stories about ordinary people who had done extraordinary things to help others. It was an enjoyable end to a special trip. He only wished that he could have more years with his wife. Fame and money counted for nothing, she and his family were his greatest treasures by far.

"For our final story this evening," announced the immaculately coiffured female presenter, "we have a heart-warming story about a boy's awful experience in the darkest days of World War Two. And though he doesn't know it, he's sitting right here in the audience."

A spotlight landed squarely on Kurt. Jessie squeezed his hand and kissed his cheek.

"Surprise!"

Overawed, Kurt made his way to the stage to be greeted and seated by the presenter as the audience clapped.

"This man, Kurt Ziegler," the woman explained, "has had an incredible life. Some of you may have read his book first published back in the forties or even have seen the movie they made of it. Born to an English mother and a German father, he was evacuated from London during the Blitz into the English countryside, to what he thought would be a place of safety. However, he found out that the woman whose house he was living in was hiding a German spy. Upon discovering that Kurt knew he was in the house, the man kidnapped Kurt and took him back to Germany. There, Kurt was placed in a special camp for members of the Hitler Youth, and told that he must go to fight on the Russian front even though he was only fifteen at that time. Kurt, would you like to share with us what happened next?"

"I decided to escape. Make my way across Germany to the Western Front."

"So that was several hundred miles across enemy territory?"

"Yes."

"What would have happened if you had been caught?"

"I would have been hung for desertion."

"And you took a friend along. Dieter."

"Yes, we did it together."

"Well, we have a wonderful surprise because we tracked down your friend, and we've flown him all the way from Germany. Come on out, Dieter!" A man who was now almost as wide as he was tall appeared on stage and ambled towards Kurt. The two men hugged and sat down on the sofa next to each other. "Dieter, I think there was something that you wanted to share with us."

"Yes, Kurt's my hero," he said in heavily accented English. "I was bullied at the camp and he befriended me. He encouraged me to go with him, and gave me the courage to do it. He literally saved my life. I'd have died if I'd stayed behind. I would have been killed by the Red Army. I was only a boy, not a soldier."

"But you both did something more, didn't you."

Dieter and Kurt looked at each other, not knowing what to say.

"These guys are clearly way too modest so let me tell you. They stowed away on a freight train for part of the journey. Inside, they found a teenage girl, Karolina, who'd managed to escape from a concentration camp. She was very weak and could barely walk. When the train was bombed, they took it in turns to carry her on their backs for over a hundred miles and across a battlefield. And when you reached the front line, you lost touch with her, isn't that so?"

"Yes, that was the last time I saw her, and I guess you too, Kurt?" said Dieter. Kurt nodded, unable to speak. His heart was in his mouth. Could it be that

Karolina had survived?

"Well, once again I have great news. We did a lot of digging and we discovered that Karolina was brought to America, and we have a video message from her son, Jan, who lives on the other side of the country in Philadelphia."

The large screen on stage filled with the face of a man.

"Hi, Kurt and Dieter. I am so glad to have this opportunity to express my gratitude. We owe everything to you. Thanks to what you did, our mom lived, married, and had four kids and six grandchildren. God bless you both. You are the reason that we are all alive. You are true heroes."

The two men wiped their eyes, carried along on the wave of emotion swirling around the studio.

"There's just one more thing," continued the presenter. "And it's the best news of all. Kurt and Dieter, tonight we have flown Karolina out here from Philadelphia."

With the audience cheering, Karolina walked on stage. She was unrecognisable. Gone was the haunted, gaunt appearance of Kurt's memory. The lady was a normal looking grandmother with her hair dyed blond, and impeccably dressed in a yellow two-piece. Beaming with joy and with eyes full of love, she embraced the two men.

"So tell us, Karolina, what was it like when you first met these guys?" asked the host once they were all seated.

"I was absolutely terrified of them. They were

wearing Hitler Youth uniforms. I thought that was it, that I'd be sent back to the concentration camp to die. But they were very sweet, and they took great care of me."

"Is there anything that you'd like to say to them after all these years."

"There are no words that can adequately describe my feelings. They risked their lives for me, carrying me across Germany. They could so easily have been caught and shot for what they did. After the horror of what I'd been through, these two restored my faith in humanity. To me, they are the best two guys in the whole world."

Prolonged clapping filled the studio.

"No, we're not. We were cowards. Karolina is the real hero here tonight." A hush descended on the audience, and the presenter moved her head back and tightened her TV smile with barely disguised concern at this totally unexpected diversion. The camera panned to Kurt. "When we got to the front line, there was a battle raging. She told Dieter and I to go on without her. She was worried that carrying her would reduce our chances of making it. Karolina was willing to sacrifice herself to let us live. And we abandoned her, left her behind. We failed to show the courage which she did. I'm so sorry, Karolina. It's something that I've regretted my entire life. As soon as we crossed the battlefield, we were taken prisoner and never knew whether you made it. Tonight I'm just so unbelievably happy to know that you lived."

The presenter quickly jumped in.

"Well folks, sounds to me like they're all heroes. That's all we've got time for tonight. Be sure to join us next week same time for another great show. And if you know of a hero living next door to you, get in touch. Have a great night."

For several days afterwards, Kurt felt as if he had won the lottery. Karolina had lived. That was such truly wonderful news. No longer need he carry the guilt that he'd left her to die. The demons from his past had all been slain, and he had finally freed the truth.

The cancer grew stronger and Kurt weaker. But he was at peace. At the end, his beloved Jessie was there holding his hand as their children stood by the bed. Kurt could no longer talk, but he hoped they could tell from the way he looked at them that they would understand how much he loved them all. Kurt counted himself a lucky man. So many of his generation had never got to experience all the happiness which he had.

When Mrs Bishop, who was over eighty by then, heard of his death, she arranged for the young vicar to hold a memorial service for Kurt. She was delighted that over thirty people attended. When the service finished, she ignored approaches from acquaintances eager to chat. There was someone who she had spotted that she was keen to talk to, seated alone on the back pew. A woman that Mrs Bishop had noticed slipping in quietly only moments before the service began. Now that same woman was standing to leave. She was already walking down the path away from the church when Mrs Bishop reached the door.

"Wait. Please wait a moment," Mrs Bishop called after her.

The woman complied. Catching up, Mrs Bishop peered at her through her big round glasses. Though so many years had passed and there was the pain of a difficult life etched on the woman's face, there was something familiar about her, something that reminded Mrs Bishop of a young girl who she had known long ago.

"Barb? Is it you?"

"Yes, it's me, Mrs Bishop."

"How lovely to see you after all this time. Thank you so much for coming. I'm sure Kurt would have appreciated it."

"It was the least that I could do."

"No, not at all dear. You were so much better than the rest of us. When we all ignored that young boy, you were there for him. A friend when he needed one."

"I must be going or I'll miss my bus. It was nice to see you. Goodbye, Mrs Bishop."

Barb gave a wistful smile and walked on and out of the churchyard.

++++++++++++++++++++++++++++++++

ALSO BY DAVID CANFORD

207

A Good Nazi? The Lies We Keep

Growing up in 1930s Germany two boys, one Catholic and one Jewish, become close friends. After Hitler seizes power, their lives are changed forever. When World War 2 comes, will they help each other, or will secrets from their teenage years make them enemies?

A Heart Left Behind

New Yorker, Orla, finds herself trapped in a web of secret love, blackmail and espionage in the build up to WW2. Moving to Berlin and hoping to escape her past, she is forced to undertake a task that will cost not only her own life but also that of her son if she fails.

Puppets of Prague

Can the dream of freedom overcome fear and oppression? Friendships are tested to the limit in this saga spanning Prague's tumultuous 20th century. In the summer of 1914 young love beckons and the future seems bright for three close friends, but momentous events throw into stark relief the differences between them that had never mattered before.

The Shadows of Seville

A gripping and moving story of loss and love, of hatred and passion, and of horror and hope, set in Spain's most evocative city during the turmoil of the Spanish Civil War and the following decades. Lose yourself in vibrant 'Sevilla' where the shadows of the past are around every corner.

Betrayal in Venice

Sent to Venice on a secret mission against the Nazis, a soldier finds his life unexpectedly altered when he saves a young woman at the end of World War Two. Discovering the truth many years later, Glen Butler's reaction to it betrays the one he loves most.

Going Big or Small

British humour collides with European culture in this tale of 'it's never too late'. Retiree, Frank, gets more adventure than he bargained for when he sets off across 1980s Europe hoping to shake up his mundane life. Falling in love with a woman and Italy has unexpected consequences.

The Throwback - The Girl who wasn't wanted

A baby's birth on a South Carolina plantation threatens to cause a scandal, but the funeral of mother and child seems to ensure that the truth will never be known. A family saga of hatred, revenge, forbidden love, overcoming hardship and helping others.

Sweet Bitter Freedom

The sequel to the Throwback. Though the Civil War has now ended, Mosa is confronted by new challenges and old adversaries who are determined to try and take what she has. While some hope to build a new South, the old South refuses to die. Will Mosa lose everything or find a way through?

Bound Bayou

A young teacher from England achieves a dream when he gets the chance to work for a year in the United States, but 1950s Mississippi is not the America he has seen on the movie screens at home. When his independent spirit collides with the rules of life in the Deep South, he sets off a chain of events he can't control.

Sea Snakes and Cannibals

A travelogue of visits to islands around the world, including remote Fijian islands, Corsica, islands in the Sea of Cortez, Mexico, and the Greek islands.

When the Water Runs Out

Will water shortage result in the USA invading Canada? One person can stop a war if he isn't killed first but is he a hero or a traitor? When two very different worlds collide, the outcome is on a knife-edge.

2045 The Last Resort

In 2045 those who lost their jobs to robots are taken care of in resorts where life is an endless vacation. For those still in work, the American dream has never been better. But is all quite as perfect as it seems?

THANK YOU

I hope you enjoyed reading Kurt's War. I would appreciate it if you could spare a few moments to post a review on Amazon. It only need be a few words.

Thanks so much,
David Canford

FREE EBOOK

Go to davidcanford.com to claim your free ebook and receive David's email newsletter including information on new book releases and promotions.

ABOUT THE AUTHOR

Writing historical fiction, David Canford is able to combine his love of history and travel in novels that take readers on a rollercoaster journey through time and place with characters who face struggle and hardship but where resilience, love and forgiveness can overcome hatred and oppression.

He has also written two novels about the future, and a travelogue.

David has three grown up daughters and lives on the south coast of England with his wife and their dog.

For more information visit DavidCanford.com or his Facebook page or Instagram. You can contact him by visiting his website.

I

Printed in Great Britain
by Amazon